Disbelief

by
J. B. Jamison

Author's Website: jbjamison.com

ImagiLearning, Inc.

ISBN 978-1-7320930-9-6

Printed in the United States

Cover design by Roy Brandt.

"Experience has shewn, that even under the best forms of government, those entrusted with power have, in time, and by slow operations, perverted it into tyranny."

Thomas Jefferson

OTHER BOOKS BY John B. Jamison

Disruption!

"A plot that unfolds at breakneck pace, rich, full characters that you want to know even more about, and more twists than the Mississippi River."

Distraction!

"My advice is to bring up several pizzas from the freezer and take the phone off the hook, you won't want to put this book down until the end!"

More at:

jamisonbooks.com

For Patty.

Chapter 1

"Put away that gun and get the hell out of my meeting!"

"I'm sorry, Mr. VanHollings, but you need to come with us please."

"What? Can't you see that I am in the middle of something here? Why are you…"

"You need to come with us, sir. Now!"

The head of security took the papers from VanHolling's hand as two other men grasped VanHolling's shoulders.

"Now look. I'm not going anywhere until someone…"

Berend VanHollings felt his feet leave the floor as the four of them moved toward the door.

Four more men were waiting in the hallway. VanHollings noticed that each of the men held a weapon.

"Would someone tell me what the hell this is about?" VanHollings said.

"I will explain when we get you to safety. Please just keep moving sir."

VanHollings was quiet as he was moved down the hallway to the elevator, down to the basement and the vehicle waiting at the alley entrance. He was placed in the rear seat between two large men with guns drawn, and looks on their faces that told him enough to just go along and let them do their jobs. He noticed a second car in front of them and a third trailing behind, each filled with armed and serious looking men. No one spoke until they arrived at VanHolling's home and led VanHollings to the windowless library that had been designated as a safe room. Moments later another group of guards escorted Mrs. VanHollings into the room.

"Berend, what is this all about?" Mrs. VanHollings said.

"I have no idea," VanHollings said as he turned to look at Raul Weith, his Chief of Security and the man who had interrupted his meeting at the office.

Weith nodded to his security team and each of them left the room to take their positions to fully secure the VanHollings home.

"You will be safe here sir," Raul said. "I am sorry for the inconvenience."

"What is going on?" VanHollings said.

"We are still assessing that sir," Weith said. "All we know at this time is that Levi Herzig was found in his office, apparently shot."

"Oh, my God!" Mrs. VanHollings said.

"Shot? When? By whom?"

"We don't know that, sir. But it looks professional. That is why we had to take the steps we have taken here sir."

"The others?" VanHollings said. "What about Ghaazi, Shuren, and the rest?"

"We don't have intel on them yet, sir. We will stay locked-down until we do have that and understand just what is actually going on, if this is just an isolated incident or something more. In the meantime, you and Mrs. VanHollings will be secure here."

"Thank you, Raul," Mrs. VanHollings said.

"Yes," VanHollings nodded, "thank you, Raul. I am sorry if I caused you any trouble. You were just doing the job I pay you to do."

"No problem sir," Weith said. "I need to go and do more of that job now. I will come back when I have more information. In the meantime, make yourselves as comfortable as you can."

"Thank you, Raul," VanHollings said as he sat on a cushioned sofa near the fireplace.

Silence.

"I think I need a drink," Mrs. VanHollings said. "How about you, dear?"

"Yes, something strong."

She handed him a glass and sat next to him on the sofa. They both drank.

"What the hell is going on?" VanHollings said. "Who is behind this?"

They watched the fire in the fireplace. Mrs. VanHollings tucked her feet, curling up on the couch like a ball.

"There's no reason to be concerned," VanHollings said. "Raul is the best there is."

"Oh, I'm not concerned," Mrs. VanHollings said.

He looked at her as they sipped from their drinks.

"You have always been the brave one, haven't you?" VanHollings said. "Even when...even when times have been...have been diffi...difficult..."

8

Silence.

"I don't..." VanHollings said. "I don't under...something is..."

"Dear?" Mrs. VanHollings said. "Are you alright?"

VanHollings looked at his wife, though she was growing blurry. Through the haze, he saw what looked like a smile on her face. Her very calm, smiling face.

"What's wrong, Berend dear?"

"What did you...did you...you?" VanHollings said looking at her, and then at the empty glass in his hand

"Yes, Berend dear. Me. With some help, of course."

"But...but...why?" He tried to sit up but could not.

"Why?" She leaned close to look into his eyes and laughed. "Why? Because, Berend my dear, you have made a mess of things. I mean, really. We used to be strong and had control of our lives. But then you did that stupid thing with the computers and had to make the deal because of that FBI woman. And now we can't do anything without asking for permission."

He could hear her, with a bit of an echo, but the room had gotten too dark to see her face.

"I mean, honestly Berend. How long did you expect me to put up with that kind of life?"

Mrs. VanHollings sipped from her glass and put it on the table.

"What's the matter dear, having a hard time seeing me now? Don't worry, it won't take much longer."

He tried to speak. He tried to reach out to grab her. Nothing happened.

"So, I decided to take matters into my own hands and reorganize things a bit. Some of the group agreed with me, while the others, well, Raul already told you about the others didn't he?"

He could not see her. He could not hear her. Everything was silent.

"Berend?" Mrs. VanHollings said.

"Berend, dear?" she said.

She got up from the sofa and straightened her dress. She took one more look to see that her husband's breathing had stopped, and then she screamed.

The door crashed open as the three guards rushed in followed by Raul Weith. He saw Berend VanHollings on the sofa and reached for a pulse.

"It must have been his heart," Mrs. VanHollings said. "The stress was just too much."

Weith shouted at the guards.

"Get the doctor! Seal the room. No one in or out until I say so. GO!"

The room emptied leaving Weith, Mrs. VanHollings, and the late Berend VanHollings.

Mrs. VanHollings reached down to take the glass from her husband's hand and handed it to Weith.

"That went well," she said.

Weith placed the empty glass in his pocket as Mrs. VanHollings placed a new glass in her husband's hand.

"Yes, ma'am," Weith said.

"And the rest is going according to schedule?"

"Yes Mrs. VanHollings, the meeting with the others is in one hour."

Mrs. VanHollings moved toward the door. She paused and turned to look at her husband.

"Pity," She said as she walked out the door.

Chapter 2

Carl Pedalton did not know he would spend the rest of the day and most of the evening helping identify the seventeen bodies, but as the rural mail carrier, he was one of the few people who knew everyone in town and could give them names. All he knew right now was that his stomach hurt from the vomiting. He was leaning against the tailgate of his truck parked at the first mailbox at the edge of town, waiting for someone from the Sheriff's office to arrive.

A patrol car pulled behind Carl's truck and Sheriff Daryl Krebel stepped out.

"What the hell is going on Carl?" Krebel said. "You sounded like a crazy man on the phone."

Carl's mouth opened but words did not come out. He just pointed to the house and nodded his head in that direction.

Krebel shook his head and started up the walk towards the small porch. Apparently, poor Carl had fallen off the wagon again, but he would have to deal with that later. He knocked on the door.

"Go on in," Carl said, "they ain't gonna answer."

The Sheriff glanced at Carl, then opened the rusty screen door and stepped inside.

"Hello? Anybody here?"

Sheriff Krebel noticed how quiet it was in the house. Then it occurred to him just how quiet it had been outside too. He peeked in the kitchen and everything looked to be as it should have been, except for the fact that it should have been breakfast time about now.

"Hello? Walt? Connie? Anybody here?"

He walked down the narrow hallway to the first door. He saw a double bed with what looked like two people under the covers. Neither of them was breathing.

"What the hell?" Krebel said.

He stepped back to avoid contaminating what had apparently become a crime scene and started toward the back of the house. He tripped over something. It was the body of the family dog.

"What the hell?"

After checking the rest of the house, he stepped back onto the porch and saw the cat. And the chickens. The quietness was beginning to make sense. He walked around the house to the small shed and found more animals, all in the same shape as the rest. Then he saw the birds lying on the ground.

"What the hell?"

Carl was standing a bit more upright when the Sheriff got back to the truck.

"What the hell happened here Carl?" Krebel said.

"It ain't just here, Daryl."

"What do you mean it ain't just here?"

"I mean they're all gone; all dead. Every last one of them."

"Yeah, I saw that," Krebel said, "damndest thing I've ever seen."

"No! The whole goddamn town," Carl said. "All of them; people, dogs..."

"What? Are you shittin' me here Carl? How'd you know?"

"I went and looked, that's how. When I found the Kellys here, I went next door to get help and that's when I found the DuChanes in the same shape. They're all like this. Every damned house in town."

Sheriff Daryl Kreble stared at Carl for a few seconds, then back at the house, then down the gravel road at the eight or nine houses that made-up Lindell, Kansas. Lindell was one of those small, unincorporated places you drove through without thinking much about; the home to people who wanted to be out here away from anyone who might stop by and interrupt their day. It was the home of seventeen people from a dozen or so families, along with a decent collection of dogs, cats, and various farm animals. Until this morning anyway. This morning they were all dead. Down to the last chicken.

Sheriff Krebel made the calls and as others arrived he directed things until someone from the Kansas State Patrol took charge, followed by people from the FBI who came all the way from Kansas City. Everyone who showed up spent the first few minutes just standing and staring down the road, trying to make sense of what had happened; how a small town was just removed from the map like this.

The first sweep revealed no clues about what had happened, who might have been involved, or how they came or went. Around lunchtime, Sheriff Krebel got into his car to head back to the office and start on his paperwork. He sat for a moment looking at the little houses lining the gravel road.

"What the hell?" he said.

Chapter 3

"Good morning Grandpa."

"Morning Ronnie, how's the kids?"

The younger man sat down in his usual chair at the table by the window. The barista smiled at the two of them and their every morning family visit. She thought it was sweet. She had no idea.

"Doin' fine. Busy as usual, running all over the place. How you doing?"

"Ah, I'm fine too. Just the usual nonsense, but what do doctors know, huh?"

"Doctors? What's wrong?"

"Nah, nothing to worry about this morning. It sounds like we have more important things to deal with don't we?"

Grandpa drank from his coffee.

"Yeah, I guess the solution they came up with after that landfill thing didn't turn out to be much of a solution after all. You saw the latest messages this morning?"

"Yes, we knew that group would never just sit back and accept things. They're too used to having their power and controlling things. At some point, they were bound to implode, but I did think it would take a bit longer than this. Herzig is the only one so far?"

"Yeah, that's all we've heard about. But some of the others have gone into hiding. Conway and Geller at least. What do you think is going on?"

Grandpa drank from his cup.

"Too early to tell," Grandpa said. "One of them might be trying to take control, or maybe some of them are working together, either is possible. But my guess is that whatever it is will happen quickly. These folks aren't known for their patience."

"Any idea who is guiding it?" Ronnie said.

"Could be any of them. None of them have any loyalty that reaches beyond their own front door. If there is ever any sign of weakness someone is going to try and take advantage of it. And the situation with the landfill certainly made the whole group look pretty weak. We'll just have to wait and see who the lead wolf is. In the meantime, you have your directions?"

"Yes," Ronnie said. "We're keeping an eye on the others to see if any of them might be at risk from this thing. Our connections are doing that now."

"Good, that's the best for now."

They both drank.

"Grandpa, there is one more thing I've heard that might be worth looking at. I'm not sure."

"What is it? About what is happening?"

"Maybe. One of my connections has heard there may be some problem in the VanHollings family, a personal problem. Something about their son, Klass. It may not be anything, but..."

"There have been some problems there for a while. VanHollings has always wanted Klass to eventually take over as head of the group, but the two of them have had, let's say, issues because of VanHollings being such an over-controlling father."

"Maybe that's what it is," Ronnie said. "Word is that there has been some kind of a split between them recently. Apparently pretty nasty. But if they've always had..."

"Have your connections look closer. It might be nothing. But then again, with this other stuff happening now, well, the timing might mean they are somehow connected."

"You think Klass might be involved in some kind of takeover against his own father?"

"Ronnie, these folks have their own definition of loyalty. Like I said, it usually stops at their own front door, but there are times when it doesn't even go that far. Check it out."

"Will do."

They drank.

"Now, are you going to tell me what that doctor thing was all about earlier?"

"Maybe tomorrow, Ronnie. Right now we have work to do."

Grandpa stood from his chair, patted his grandson on the shoulder, winked at the barista, and walked out the door.

Chapter 4

"Agent Graham, this is a surprise. Is there something I can do for you?"

Emily had just stepped from her boat when she heard the familiar voice.

"And good morning to you Dr. Mercer," Emily said. "I just thought we would come out and see if we could offer you any assistance in serving the warrants."

"Well, thank you very much, Agent Graham," Dr. Jeri Mercer said, "but I believe we have things well under control here. That is unless you have another of those magical letters like the one you brought to St. Louis?"

"No," Emily said. "No letter. I just thought that since you haven't spent that much time out here in the bayous we might be able to offer you some local insight, maybe help out a little, you know?"

"How nice. But I believe my team from homeland can handle things, along with our friends we've brought from the Federal Marshall's office."

"I just thought that..."

"While we haven't spent as much time out here in the swamps as you have," Mercer smiled, "I assure you we are prepared for whatever we might find here. I'm sure you have better things to do this morning."

"Okay. Do you mind if Agent Velazquez and I just hang out and observe? This might be a good opportunity for him to see how things are done."

"As much as I would love to help you train your team, Graham, our plans do not include room for any observers. I suggest you get back into your little boat and go find something else to do. Some other time, okay?"

"Sure, no problem," Emily said. She paused. "So, you're planning on sending the team up the path there, the one to the East?"

"Yes, that gives us the best approach. But if our cover is broken we have a second team staging at the East side of the target, since that's the direction they are most likely to try and escape."

"You think they'll run to the East?"

"That's where they have another boat dock. Look, Graham, I don't mean to be rude but we really do have a mission to complete. If I need to I can make a phone call and..."

"No, that's fine," Emily said. "It looks like you have things well under control here so Agent Velazquez and I will be on our way. Good luck with your mission."

Dr. Mercer was already gone.

Emily got into the boat as Carlos Velazquez pushed it from the muddy bank.

"What was that all about?" Velazquez said.

"I never told you about her? Oh, she's just an old friend I met once up in St. Louis. She apparently holds grudges."

Emily guided the little boat along the maze of channels in the bayou West of Houma, Louisiana, some sixty miles SouthWest of New Orleans.

"You come out this far very often?" Velazquez said.

"Not so much anymore. Just once in a while for work. I used to come out a lot, back when I first moved down."

"You must have...hey, isn't that the way we came in, over there?" Valazquez said.

"We aren't going back yet. We have work to do."

After a few minutes and more than a few turns through the overgrown grasses, Emily pulled the boat up against a muddy piece of land.

"Now we walk," Emily said.

"Walk? Out here?"

Emily looked at Velazquez.

"You've never been out here? Really?"

"Well, a little, yeah. But not clear out here, not out of the boat anyway."

Emily stepped into the water.

"Make sure your boots are tight. The mud will suck 'em right off."

She disappeared into the tall grass.

Velazquez checked his boots, slowly stepped into the mud, and followed.

"Where we going, anyway?" Velazquez said.

"To serve a warrant," Emily said.

"What? Where?"

"South."

They walked in silence.

"Hey, are there any crocodiles out here?" Velazquez said.

"Crocs? Out here? No way. You'll find them over in Florida, but not around here."

"Good."

Silence.

"Lots of gators though."

Velazquez stopped.

"Gators? But you just said..."

"Yeah, both gators and crocs in Florida, but we just have the gators. You do know they're not the same thing, don't you?"

"I do now."

"Just keep moving. If you stand still for very long you're either going to sink in the muck or the fire ants will get you. And don't worry about the gators. They'll hear us coming and stay far out of the way."

Silence as they walked.

"But," Emily said, "what you do need to watch for are the snakes. We got snakes out here that, if one gets you, you've got maybe twenty minutes to get to the hospital. And we're a lot farther away than that. So don't worry about gators."

"Shit," Velazquez said as he started walking again.

"Carlos!" Emily said. "I have never heard you use language like that before."

"I've never been out here before."

"Relax," Emily stopped walking. "This is as far as we're going."

Carlos looked around the small clearing.

"What's here?"

"There, under that brush piled up there, see that boat?"

"Yeah. What's that doing there?" Velazquez said.

"Just get ready," Emily said. "You get behind that tall grass there. And you might want to have your gun out."

"Gun? What the hell is going on?"

He heard them coming through the mud.

"Shhhh..." Emily said. "Get ready."

Emily was behind the brush pile and Velazquez was behind the grass when the two men came into the clearing, breathing hard. They moved towards the brush pile.

"Good morning there Adrien," Emily said as she stood. "Going fishing?"

"Em!" Adrien said.

Adrien Cambre glanced around looking for a direction to run.

"Now don't run off on me here," Emily said. "I'd hate to have to order Carlos to shoot you or something."

Emily nodded towards Velazquez as he stepped from the tall grass.

"What choo doin' out here in da mud dis erly in da mornin'?" Adrien said.

"Well, it seems you've got a warrant or something Adrien," Emily said. "And I figured you were too smart to let those city agents get you, so Carlos and I decided to help them out a bit."

"How'd you know we was gonna run down dis a-way?

"You remember that time you took me out hunting snappers? You showed me your boat you hid out here South of your camp."

Adrien looked at his escape boat, still under the brush.

"Yeah," Adrien said. "Fergot 'bout dat."

"Who's your friend?" Emily said.

"Oh, dis here's Kevin Tassin, from up Thibodaux way," Adrien said. "He a good boy. Won't give you no trouble."

"Nice to meet you, Kevin," Emily said. "Looks like you picked a miserable morning to visit."

Emily looked at Adrien.

"Well, why don't we start our way back? Adrien, you and Kevin lead the way? Carlos and I will follow along behind."

The four followed the path that Adrien and Kevin had just made from the house. As they entered the camp clearing they saw the collection of agents standing by the house. There were a lot of them, with a lot of gear and equipment. One of the Homeland Security people noticed them and a few seconds later Dr. Jeri Mercer was walking towards Adrien, Kevin, Carlos, and Emily.

"Agent Velazquez?" Emily said.

"Yeah?"

"You might want to take some notes. I think you are about to get a really good lesson on how this inter-agency relations stuff actually works."

Chapter 5

"Ok, just what part of not shedding any blood did you all seem to misunderstand? Seventeen people? Seventeen? The articles of war are perfectly clear that we will avoid bloodshed, and when we do have to take lives we do not kill productive citizens. Even those who stand to fight against us are given the opportunity to yield and join us before being killed. Thirty-seven? Would someone care to explain to me why this has happened?"

The group was silent, each man looking at his shoes.

"No one has an answer?" Ethan Landry continued. "So when I talk with Klass and have to explain why someplace in the middle-of-nowhere Kansas may have just destroyed our entire mission, I just tell him that, what, something went wrong and we accidentally killed seventeen people, along with a bunch of dogs, cats, farm animals, and birds? Birds!"

Landry looked around the group.

"Is that what I say?"

"The pulse was too high."

"What?" Landry said. "Who said that?"

Jimmy Sanders looked up.

"I did. The pulse was strong enough to disrupt the electrical impulses in the bodies, which isn't what we wanted to do."

"You think?" Landry said.

"Either we miscalculated," Danny Whitley said, "or used the wrong configuration on the device."

Landry looked at Jimmy and Danny, then around the rest of the group.

"So, which was it?" Landry said. "Miscalculation or misconfiguration? Which?"

"We don't know yet," Danny said. "But we will find out and fix it."

"Do that!"

Chapter 6

Reinhold Geller had learned to scuba dive when he was fourteen years old. He had tried it on a family vacation to Australia and was hooked. He had enjoyed diving the most beautiful sites in the world, many of them from his eighty-four-foot yacht he named Tiefes Wasser, or Deep Water. This morning the Tiefes Wasser was in the blue waters near Belize, floating above a dive that Geller had wanted to explore for a very long time. The large reef led to a wall, essentially an underwater cliff that led down into the dark blue of whatever the true depths of the ocean held. Even using his best nitrox gear, Geller would only be able to explore a little more than one hundred feet of the wall. His dream was that, someday, he would go further. As Geller rolled into the water, his diving partner, the head of his security detail and a long time friend, followed him in. The water was warm and almost perfectly clear. While the reef was one of the most beautiful he had ever seen, Geller headed for the wall and the thrill of floating above the abyss. For Reinhold, this was as much of a religious experience he ever experienced.

The two divers saw the edge of the reef and the misty blue water that stretched beyond. As they reached the edge and looked down, the misty blue became darker and darker, still clear, and still unreachable. The dive partners double-checked their gear, moved to the edge, and started down. As the light decreased, the sea life changed, making this a very different place than the top of the reef. Geller was fascinated by the changes he saw taking place in front of him. He took photos and pointed out interesting things to his partner who was always nearby. Far too soon Geller saw his depth gauge read one-hundred feet, the place where bad things could happen very quickly. The nitrox helped avoid things like narcosis, the mental confusion and sometimes convulsions that occurred when the pressures of depth altered gasses in the blood. The confusion could lead to a diver making a mistake. Mistakes could lead to very bad things. But Geller was experienced enough to realize the dangers, and his limitations, and knew he had to settle for no more than descending another ten or twenty feet before heading back to the reef. He was aware of the dangers and focused his remaining time on that amazing wall so he missed nothing.

What Reinhold Geller did not see was his dive partner swimming up closer to him. Geller did not see the knife. The first distraction from the wall was the pain, which he immediately thought was a cramp. Until he saw the blood. And felt a second pain.

Slowly, Geller began to realize the dream he had carried for so many years. As he drifted deeper, the darkness increased, as did the blueness. He thought it was beautiful. It almost swept away the pain. Darker. Bluer. He saw his dive partner now floating above him, just floating there, becoming smaller and smaller. Geller felt the increasing pressure but could not take his eyes off of the wall where he saw things he had never, ever seen before. He drifted down until all that was left was the murky blueness that stretched into whatever lived below the wall.

Chapter 7

"Good morning gentlemen," Adriana VanHollings said. "I appreciate your adjusting your schedules for this call."

Polite greetings from the others on the line.

"Let me begin by making sure everyone is here. Hue?"

"Yes, I'm here," Hue Shuren said.

"Fine. Elton?"

"Good morning," Elton Mann said.

"Sebastian, are you with us?" Adriana said.

"Yes," Sebastian Alvarado said.

"Polachev?"

"I am here," Polachev Savelievich said.

"Very good. And Farvad, how about you?"

"I am here as well," Farvad Ghaazi said.

"Excellent. Then let us get started. I simply wanted to let you all know that…"

"Wait," Huo Shuren said. "What about the others? Herzig, Geller, and Conway? Why are they not here?"

"Yes," Adriana VanHollings said. "I spoke with each of them just as I spoke with each of you and explained the new direction we were planning on taking with the group. Unfortunately, I am afraid that Mr. Herzig, Mr. Geller, and Mr. Conway did not agree with that new direction and they each decided they would no longer participate in our group."

"What do you mean…?" Farvad Ghaazi said.

"Why would they…? Hue Shuren said.

"Gentlemen," Adriana said. "As we talked earlier, we knew this might be a possibility because of the scope of the changes we are making. It is unfortunate, and I know we will miss their participation. However, I assure you that this does not alter our plans in any way."

"But this is a problem," Sebastian Alvarado said. "This could be very dangerous because of what they know about us."

"Yes," Polachev Savelievich said. "There will be…"

"Gentlemen. Gentlemen! There is no danger, I assure you."

"But what if one of them decides to talk?" Faraad Ghaazi said. "Or what if they decide to work together against us?"

"That is not going to happen," Adriana said.

"You do not know that," Polachev Savelievich said.

"Yes, gentlemen," Adriana said. "I do know for a fact that we have nothing to fear from Mr. Herzig, Mr. Geller, or Mr. Conway. Nothing at all."

"What about any of the others?" Elton Mann said. "That FBI Agent, for example? She knows enough to cause some real problems for us if she thinks we're breaking that deal your husband agreed too."

"Agent Graham, you mean? No, she will not be a problem for us. In fact, she may turn out to be of great help to us. I will be looking into that tomorrow and let you know. And if anyone else tries to cause problems, we'll deal with those just as we are the rest. Relax gentlemen, a new day lies ahead."

"What about your son?" Polachev Savelievich said.

Silence.

"My son? Yes. That is being taken care of as well."

Chapter 8

Daryle Krebel never liked it anytime the state and federal folks showed up. Whenever they came in, his investigation became their investigation and none of them made much of an apology for it. Most of the time they wouldn't even talk to him, let alone update him on what was going on. But this afternoon, as Sheriff Krebel parked along the gravel road outside of Lindell, he was relieved to see all those other folks there.

Daryl had never planned on becoming a Sheriff. In fact, he really didn't like the title. It made him think about boots with spurs, a shiny silver badge, and two guys with six guns facing each other in an empty street waiting for the other to draw. He preferred law enforcement officer, or even cop, though neither of those had been in his plans either. It all started that afternoon he and the judge had decided that going into the military was better than a cell, and the next day Daryl found himself at boot camp. Somehow, he ended up in the Military Police, followed by a couple of undercover roles that led to his being picked to take part in even more interesting things that did not officially exist. He ended up building a respectable reputation and twenty years later found himself back in Wichita trying to figure out what to do next. With his background, he could have had his pick of good jobs there, but he was tired. He had spent enough time dealing with crooks and liars and wanted to just spend some time doing something calmer. Something boring. He heard about the opening for Sheriff over near someplace called Lindell and it sounded like paradise. And it was. Until today.

Daryl got out of his car and walked up to the yellow tape and the people standing there. He disliked gawkers even more than experts. He hated them even more than the press. At least the press had a reason for being there. He smiled as he realized that today neither of those were his problem. Not with all of those state and federal cars parked on the road.

"Sheriff Krebel?" the voice came from somewhere across the yellow tape.

At least they were talking to him.

"Yeah, I'm Krebel," He said as he ducked under the tape.

"Andy Bradley from the FBI. Can we speak with you for a few minutes? Over here?"

Daryl had a bad feeling that this conversation might end up with his having to deal with gawkers and press after all.

"Sure. Whatever you need."

Daryl followed Agent Bradley to a large trailer with more people inside gathered around maps and satellite images on a lot of screens.

"Sheriff," Bradley said, "we need your opinion on something here."

"Sure. And you can just call me Daryl."

"Right. We're looking at possible ways whoever did this might have gotten in and back out. The maps show the road here, Twenty-Two, as the only way to get in and out of Lindell. You know this area. Are there any other ways someone could have come in?"

Daryl glanced at the maps.

"Nope," Daryl said, "Twenty-two is the only road. I guess they could have come in across country, though that's unlikely."

"Why is that?" Someone asked. "It looks level enough to cross."

"Yeah, well, it looks level on the maps," Daryl said. "but those don't show all the holes, and gullies, and the fences. Nah, if someone came here other than Twenty-two they would have to be local to know the way, and I'm guessing whatever happened here wasn't local."

Conversations around the room.

"Have you got any idea yet of just what did happen here?" Daryl asked.

"I understand you were military, right?" Andy Bradley said.

"Yeah,"

"Have you ever heard of something called an electro-magnetic-pulse? It's a…"

"EMP?" Daryl said. "You think this was some kind of EMP thing? Out here?"

"It is a possibility," Bradley said. "We have no idea just what it was for sure, but the impact is what we would expect from an EMP, yes."

"What the hell," Daryl said.

"Well, thanks for the time, Sheriff," Agent Bradley said.

"Sure, no problem."

Daryl started toward the door and back to his role as observer.

"Hey, Daryl?" Agent Bradley said.

"Yeah?"

"I would really appreciate it if you would stick around a while, and just go out and kind of look around the area since you are familiar with it. Let us know if you find anything or have any ideas at all."

"Sure, whatever I can do to help."

Daryl smiled as he stepped from the trailer. Gawkers and press were somebody else's problem today.

Chapter 9

Emily grabbed a napkin from the container and reached for the shrimp poorboy on her plate when she felt the vibration from her phone. It had been a very long day and she was tempted to just let it go and enjoy her sandwich but she glanced at the number more out of habit than dedication. It said 'Dasilva'.

"To what do I owe the honor of..." Emily said.

"What the hell did you do?" Arturo Dasilva said.

"I don't..."

"My phone hasn't stopped ringing. I've gotten calls from Homeland, the U. S. Marshal's Office, even a senator. A SENATOR, Graham. What the hell did you do?"

Em felt her muscles tense, and her knuckles turned white around her phone.

"Are you listening to me, Graham?"

"Yeah, I'm listening. It must be about this morning. The little thing with Dr. Mercer?"

"Little? Graham, you need to look that word up in the dictionary. They're calling for your skin Graham. That's how little it is."

"Oh come on," Emily said. "All we did was..."

"It doesn't matter what you did, Graham. What matters is that you have given these people a reason to get even with you for everything else you've ever done to them, and they're going for it."

"But, it was just..."

"Stop!"

Silence.

"Look, Emily, we've talked before about this. That attitude you have that makes you so damned smart is also the thing that gets you in the most trouble. And this time its trouble with a capital T. Jeez, Em, a senator?"

Silence.

"I think I have it calmed down for now," Dasilva said. "But you need to stay quiet for a while. I mean anytime your brain tries to send something to your mouth you have to stop it! Understand?"

"Okay."

Click.

Emily looked at the sandwich on her plate and hesitated. Could she eat anything at all with her stomach tied in knots from the call?

Yes, she could.

Chapter 10

Angelique Fanchon Decourdreau had not slept since the drums had awakened her at three o'clock. They were loud, and they spoke a rhythm she had never heard before. There were no words, just the sound of drums if they were being beaten by hail falling from the sky. No pattern. No meaning. She had spent the past hours with her cards, but the Tarot spoke with that same meaningless voice, giving cards that refused to offer a meaningful message. No matter what she tried, the only thing Angelique found was chaos. She had even begun to wonder if all of her belief in these things might be faulty. Suddenly, Angelique began to understand the actual message was just that. It was chaos. Something was coming that threatened to bring full and complete chaos, leading people to question the very beliefs they had built their lives on. What was it? Where was it from? Who was bringing it?

But now that she understood the message, she began to calm her mind once again and find that source inside her that might connect herself with the answers. She held the cards in her hand, slowly sliding through the deck, and pulled the card.

It was a queen. The same queen that many months ago had spoken of Emily Graham. Now Angelique knew where she should begin her search for answers.

Chapter 11

Hector Conway was a man of routines. It was one of the many traits he had gotten from his mother. Hector's father was an unpredictable man, heavy with drink and with his anger. Routine was how Hector's mother made her world survivable, and how she protected her children. Even now, fifty years after his mother died and Hector had run from his old man's fists, the routine served as the one safe piece of his life. Up at six, shower, shave, dressed, breakfast of half a grapefruit, two fried eggs, and coffee, and the newspaper. There were many other more up-to-date sources for the news, but this was about routine, so as Hector stepped from bed this morning he knew the paper would be waiting at his breakfast table.

The shower would be hot. Not too hot. Just enough to make him briefly hold his breath when he stepped in. Shampoo was first, then soap. The entire shower would take seven minutes. Routine. Hector knew it was this routine that had made him the man he was. Others wasted time, hesitated too often, became distracted. That was his father's way. Not his.

The bedroom door opened and two men entered. One was Roger Wydler, Conway's head of security, and the other was Nicholas, Conway's personal barber. Nicholas Tassou's father was the barber who had given Hector his first haircut so many years ago, so it just seemed right to offer him the job when it came up. It made sense. Part of life's routine.

"I'm really sorry about this Nick," Roger Wydler said, "but I need to check your stuff there. We have some problems going on and we're checking everything really closely now. I have to do it. I'm really sorry."

"Don't worry about it Roger," the barber said. "I understand. Here you go. Whatever you need to do."

"Yeah, thanks. It just feels wrong doing it. I mean, you've been around here longer than any of us."

Roger opened the little bag and pulled everything out onto the table. He opened bottles, squeezed a bit out of each tube, looked closely at the razor and strap, looking for anything that might be out of the routine.

"Here you go Nick, I'm really sorry."

Seven minutes after stepping into the shower Hector came back into the bedroom wearing his robe.

"What are you sorry about Roger?" Conway said.

"Aw, it just didn't feel right having to search through Nick's stuff like that."

"Nick's stuff? You searched his bag? What the hell are you doing that for?"

"Well, the orders are to…"

"I don't care about any orders. Nick is like part of the family here. Don't do it again, understand?"

"Yes sir," Roger said. "I'll pass the word."

"Okay then. I'm sorry Nick. Now, let's get started, we're behind schedule."

Hector sat in the chair as Nicholas spread the towel around his shoulders and went to work. Hector closed his eyes to make himself adjust to the disrupted schedule. Roger leaned against the bedroom door and watched as Nick combed and dried Conway's hair and then began the shave. It was the same every morning. Routine. Nicholas took the tube of shaving cream from his bag, then turned his head and coughed slightly.

"Catching a cold there Nick?" Roger said.

"Nah, just something in my throat. Haven't had my coffee yet." They smiled.

What Roger did not know was that the cough had covered the sound of the small glass vial breaking as Nicholas squeezed the tube. What Roger had found earlier when he opened that tube was plain old shaving cream. But mixed with the contents of the little vial, the tube was now filled with something very different. Nicholas squeezed some of the gel into his hands and began rubbing it onto Hector's face.

Same thing every morning. Routine.

Until.

Hector Conway opened his eyes. He tried to say something.

"Need something, Mr. Conway?" Roger said as he moved from the door.

"I…I…can't…"

Nicholas Tassou stepped back from the chair as Roger rushed up. The head of security reached for his radio.

"Code Black. I repeat. Code Black. Master Bedroom."

Roger grabbed Conway's arms as he slid from the chair, and eased him to the floor. He checked pulse, respiration, and saw the perspiration on Conway's bright red face. The door crashed open and more of the security detail came in with the doctor. Maintaining a routine was no longer on anyone's mind.

It was over as quickly as it had begun. The doctor tried several things. Injections, CPR, antidotes, anything and everything that should have helped. The room grew quiet as they all stopped and realized what had just happened. It was then that Roger remembered Nicholas Tassou, the almost member of the family.

"Tassou!" Roger said. "Where is he?"

They found Nick in a chair next to the bed. The chemicals that had been absorbed through Conway's face had also made their way through Nick's hands. He knew they would, which is why he had found the chair. He could have just wiped the stuff off, but this was better than what they would have done to him if he had lived. There was a smile on Nick's face. He knew Conway's routine, and his last thought had been about the newspaper that was sitting next to the eggs on the breakfast table.

Chapter 12

"Well, you were right Grandpa. Things are happening quickly."

"Yes, Ronnie. Their lack of patience will come back to bite them one of these days. First, it was Herzig, then VanHollings, and then Reinhold Geller, all in twenty-four hours."

"Well, VanHollings was a heart attack, so I'm not sure…"

"A heart attack is not always a heart attack Ronnie."

"You think it wasn't?"

"It's just the timing. If he was the only one, then maybe. But not like this. No, someone is leading a takeover of the group and these men had to be removed."

"Who?"

"That's the question, isn't it?" Grandpa said.

"Who is left?" Ronnie said. "Hue Shuren? Sebastian Alvarado? Neither of them seems the type to do something like this on their own. Farvad Ghaazi? Maybe. Elton Mann? Doubtful. Polachev Savelievich? Perhaps."

Grandpa drank from his coffee.

"What about VanHolling's son Klass?" Ronnie said. "Like we said yesterday…"

"Yes, but what is happening would take a lot of resources, and I'm not sure Klass has gotten that strong yet. It must be one of the members, or there is someone else."

"Someone from outside the group?" Ronnie said.

"Just someone else. Someone other than the five we know about. We need to look around and see who else might have this kind of influence."

"I'll get that started."

They drank from their coffee and glanced out the window at the traffic outside.

"You said you would tell me about the doctors today," Ronnie said.

"Later. Have we heard anything new about Kansas? That EPM thing?"

"EMP, Grandpa."

"Means the same to me either way," Grandpa said.

"It's electro-magnetic pulse. Think of it like a bolt of lightning you could use like a weapon to destroy electrical things, but not the people around them. You could shut-down all communications, computers, anything electrical. Pretty much leave your enemy in the dark."

"Okay, I've read about those. But, don't they need something like a nuke to work? To generate that kind of energy?"

"The big ones, yeah. The media talks about what would happen if someone used a nuclear EMP, maybe Korea, or China. But while that could possibly happen sometime, the real threat is from the smaller ones. Some of them are small enough to carry around with you? Heck, you can find the instructions to build one online, and even order all of the parts too."

"The world has gone insane," Grandpa said. "So that's what happened in Kansas? Somebody drove up with a briefcase and zapped that town? I thought it wasn't supposed to kill anyone?"

"It would have had to be something bigger than a briefcase EMP, and yeah, they did something wrong, too. Apparently, the pulse was too strong. We don't know if that was an accident, or intentional."

"I'll be glad to get out of this role."

"Wait," Ronnie said, "What do you mean, out? Is this about the doctors?"

Grandpa drank from his coffee.

"Yeah," Grandpa said, "but don't go getting all fired-up about it. These doctors aren't as smart as they think they are."

"What did they say?"

"Well, it's my heart."

"Heart!"

"Now there you go. Just stop it."

"What about your heart? What did they say?"

"Its nothing new. I've had a few, um, what do they call them? Episodes, that's it. I've had a few episodes over the years, you've known about those."

"Yeah, have they gotten worse?"

"I don't think so. I just think the doctors need to make another payment on their timeshares in Boca."

"Come on. What is going on?"

"Well, they say my heart is just getting weaker and that I need to slow down. Stay away from stress, and give up my daily shot of whiskey. Like that's going to happen, the one bright spot of my day. No offense intended."

"So that means…"

"It means nothing. I'm not about to sit at home and stare out the window or at some television screen, and I sure as hell am not going to join some bridge club or spend the day in some bar. Well, maybe the bar wouldn't be that bad if they keep the jukebox turned down."

"Come on. This is serious."

"Yes, it is. What we are doing here is serious. This is what I need to be doing, and having you be a part of it with me takes away the stress. Ronnie, I told you that first day we talked about our group that it is bigger than we are. I can't just walk away from it. I can't."

Silence.

"I understand Grandpa."

"I know you do. That's why I picked you. Now is there anything else we need to talk about this morning?"

"Like I told you yesterday, we've been watching to see if any of the other folks we know are having any issues."

"And?"

"It looks like there is something going on with Emily Graham, that FBI agent that has been…"

"I remember her. What's going on? Is she in danger?"

"Not in danger health-wise, as far as we know. But there is a lot of conversation going on about her up in places that would normally not be concerned about an individual agent. Something has gotten their attention and it doesn't appear to be slowing down."

"Do we need to distract it?" Grandpa said.

"Not yet, at least I don't think so. But we'll keep an eye on it."

"Keep an eye on those folks around her then too. We still don't know where this mess is going."

Grandpa reached for his coffee and stopped. He closed his eyes.

"Grandpa? You okay?"

Grandpa opened his eyes, took a deep breath, and drank from his cup.

"Never better."

"Was that one of those…"

"Have a great day Ronnie. Gotta run. Things to do. Give the kids a hug from Grandpa."

Chapter 13

Emily turned from Leon C. Simon Drive onto the short driveway to the gate. The guard stepped out of the shack as she stopped.

"Morning Del," she said.

"Good morning Agent Graham. I'm sorry, but you'll need to wait here a moment."

"What's going on? Gate stuck again or something? I thought we fixed that."

"Just a minute Agent Graham. Someone will be here shortly. I'm sorry."

"Sorry for what? And what's with the Agent Graham thing Del? Why so formal."

"I am sorry Ma'am. I really am."

"What..."

Emily noticed two people walking up to the gate from inside. One of the men was Arturo Dasilva, the other was Carlos Velazquez.

"What is going on here?" Emily said as Dasilva walked to her car. "I didn't get word you were coming. What is it, some kind of surprise inspection or something?"

"We need to talk Graham," Dasilva said. "Please step out of the car."

"Alright," Emily said as she stepped out. "Just what the hell is going on here? I can take a joke..."

She glanced at Velazquez but he stared at the ground.

"I'm sorry Graham," Dasilva said. "This is no joke. I am here to inform you that you are officially under suspension. You are no longer..."

"Suspension? You are kidding me. Is this about that thing yesterday with Mercer?"

"Graham, all I know is that I was told to get on a plane and be hear this morning to inform you of the decision. It came from somewhere above my pay grade, so I don't know what is behind it. You are under suspension, effective immediately. I'll need your badge please."

"My badge? Oh, come on Arturo, this is just insane."

"It is what it is Graham, and I'm not enjoying this any more than you are. We've had our issues in the past, but I've always thought that if I needed someone to be there in a pinch, you were who I would call. Badge please."

"Emily took her badge in her hand, glanced at it, and handed it to Agent Dasilva. The others standing nearby all looked at their shoes.

"And your gun."

Silence.

Emily felt the vibration from her phone.

"Emily, your gun please."

She handed Dasilva her gun.

The phone vibrated.

"And now, we will escort you…"

The phone vibrated. Emily looked at it and saw Torchwood.

"Now?" Emily said, and then looked at Dasilva. "Just a minute. I need to take this."

"Graham!" she said into the phone.

"Emily, this is Linda, at Torchwood. How soon could you get here?"

"Get there? Is there a problem?"

"Well, your dad is having a very difficult morning this morning, more difficult than usual."

"Okay. What's going on?"

"Well, he's pretty upset, and it got physical for a while. It was mostly about the shoes again, and that's not happened for a while now, you know?"

"He got physical again?"

"I'm afraid I had to have the security guys come down again. They are in with him now."

Emily paused. She thought about her dad, she thought about Dasilva holding her badge and gun in his hand, she thought about Dr. Jeri Mercer, and she thought about the definition of 'difficult morning'.

"Emily?" Linda said.

"Yeah, I'm here. Okay, I understand. I will get there as soon as I can."

"Thanks, Emily. I'm sorry to bother you like this. I hope the rest of your morning is going okay."

"It's going somewhere, that's for sure. Thanks, Linda."

Emily put her phone in her pocket.

"As I was saying," Dasilva said. "We will escort you in so you can get the things from your office and..."

Emily put one hand in the air like a crossing guard at the school crosswalk.

"I'll tell you what, Super Agent Dasilva. I'll just make this simpler for everyone. Why don't you just put everything in a big cardboard box and send it to me? Unless it is important to somebody up there that I do some kind of walk-of-shame in front of everyone in the building. Is that important?"

"No, it isn't," Dasilva said. "We'll send everything to you."

"You are so kind," Emily said as she looked again to Velazquez. His stare did not move from the ground. She looked again at Dasilva.

"So, am I free to go, or do you need my jacket with the logo on it? Or maybe my pants?"

"You can go," Dasilva said. "And Emily, I am really..."

She was already backing out of the drive and turning to go West on Leon C. Simon Drive.

Chapter 14

"I hope you are calling to tell me you have found the problem and fixed it," Klass VanHollings said.

"Yes, we have," Ethan Landry said. "It was a miscalculation of…"

"Spare me the details and just tell me that it will not happen again. Tell me that we are ready to move."

"We are ready to move," Landry said.

"Excellent! Is the first truck ready to go?"

"Yes."

"Then give the order," Klass said, "and let the holy war begin! This is the beginning of a new era, my friend. You and your soldiers there will be remembered as heroes of the faith."

"We are just doing what we can to serve," Landry said.

"Very soon," Klass said, "our nation will finally become what it was intended to become. The home of the one, true faith. A land dedicated to the one, true word of the Lord, and the one, true people of God. It took God six days to create the world, and he will do it again now. Six more days and the dream will become a reality!"

"That has been our prayer," Landry said.

"How long before the device is in place?"

"It will be in the city tomorrow morning, ready for the implementation tomorrow afternoon. It's a long drive and we…"

"One more day is nothing to God, my friend," Klass VanHollings said. "Nothing at all."

Chapter 15

The hallway was quiet as Emily walked to the nurse's station.

"Hi Linda, I got here as quick as I could. How is he?"

"Oh, hi Emily," Nurse Linda Despre said, "I was just getting ready to call you. The security guys got him talking and laughing and he settled back down again. I just checked on him and he was sleeping. I'm sorry I didn't catch you and save you the trip out here."

"No, that's okay," Emily said. "What happened?"

"It was his shoes again."

"Those damn shoes. I'm really sorry."

"No, it's okay. It happens a lot with dementia. We never know what their mind is going to get stuck on. With him, it's those shoes. But Emily, there is something this time."

"What?"

"He got really worked-up this time and his BP went sky-high. His sugar levels got all out of line too. And what concerns me is that they're not settling back down as quickly as we'd like."

"Okay."

"We're watching him, but I need to tell you that if we don't see things improving on their own we may have to send him over to the hospital where they can deal with it."

"I understand. This has happened before, hasn't it?" Emily said.

"Yes, but as things progress it gets harder and harder for everything to stabilize on their own. I just wanted you to be aware that we may have to take other steps. I didn't want you to be surprised."

"So, he's getting worse?" Emily said.

"Well, there hasn't really been any change in his illness. But these episodes take their toll on the entire body, and the longer they go on the weaker he gets, and the harder it is to recover each time."

"I understand," Emily said.

"You just need to be prepared, Emily. He might come out of this just fine and keep the security guys busy for a long time..."

"But, maybe not, right?"

"We'll do everything we can here."

"I know you will. Can I go in for a bit?"

"Absolutely, let me know if you need anything."

Emily stood next to the bed watching the quiet up and down of the blanket as he slept. Her eyes did not move as she sat in the chair and her mind raced in dozens of different directions.

"We'll do everything we can..." Linda had said.

Everything we can.

She closed her eyes.

When she opened them he was looking right at her.

"What's the matter, babe?" He said. "What's wrong?"

His eyes were clear. He looked like Dad.

"Nothing," Emily said, I was just sitting here for a bit.

"Nah, you had the same look on your face you did that day you were in, what, the fourth grade? You came home from school after those girls had talked you into doing something you didn't want to do and you felt bad about it. What was that girl's name again?"

"Rebecca," Emily said. "Good grief, I had almost forgotten about that."

"Yeah, Rebecca. You walked in the house and flopped down on the couch...had that same look on your face and said something about how it was all so unfair. So, tell me what's wrong? Rebecca isn't back is she?"

"No, dad, it's not Rebecca."

Emily tried to think of where to begin to explain her morning. How she had just had her world crushed by some vindictive doctor-woman she had only met twice in her life. It made no sense to her at all, so how could she explain it to him?

"Her folks ran that store downtown, didn't they?" Dad said.

"Her? Oh, you mean Rebecca? Yeah, by the restaurant."

"Yeah, I remember them now."

Dad sat up on the side of the bed and glanced around the room. He looked at Emily.

"They stole my shoes again this morning. Did you know that?"

That quickly.

"What, Dad?" Emily said.

"My shoes, them sons-a-bitches stole them again. They didn't think I saw them, but I did. I need you to go out there and get my shoes so I can go throw a couple of those ass-holes off this boat! Go ahead. They've got em out there somewhere! Go get 'em!"

One idea to try.

"Okay," Emily said, "I'll go see if I can find them. Why don't you lay back down for a few minutes while I do that?"

"I'm not going to sleep, I'm going to…"

"No, not sleep. Just lay back down so they won't suspect we're up to anything."

"Yeah, good idea. Just go get those shoes. I paid three hundred dollars for those shoes. Had 'em made special for me."

He put his head on the pillow and pulled up the blanket.

"Close your eyes so they don't suspect anything," Emily said, "I'll be back as soon as I get the shoes."

Emily stood outside the door until she heard his snoring and then walked to her car.

Chapter 16

Sheriff Daryl Kreble had only been gone for a couple of hours, but when he walked back up to the yellow tape he saw that things had changed. There were more vehicles and trailers, some of them looked military, and the people guarding the tape carried weapons.

"I'm sorry sir," one of the guards said as Daryl approached, "there are no unauthorized personnel allowed in the area."

Daryl showed his badge.

"I believe if you speak with Agent Bradley you'll find I am one of those authorized personnel you mentioned."

"One moment sir, please wait here," the guard said before he spoke into his radio.

A few minutes later Daryl saw Agent Bradley approach.

"I'm sorry for that Sheriff," Bradley said, "but as you can see, there have been some changes here, along with changes in command."

"It looks like it," Daryl said. "I just thought I might take another look…"

"I'm sorry, but that won't be possible. You see…"

Bradley paused and nodded to the guard who stepped away. Bradley looked over his shoulder at the crowd still growing behind him, then at Krebel.

"Shit, Daryl," Agent Bradley said, "everything has changed here now. Do you know what I've been doing for the past two hours? Chasing gawkers off the fence, that's what I've been doing. Gawkers!"

Bradley looked at the ground.

"Who's running the show now?" Daryl said.

"Hell if I know. They don't tell me anything anymore. There's so many suits and uniforms here now…I don't know what the hell really happened here last night, but whatever it is has made a lot of people nervous."

Bradly looked at Daryl.

"I'm sorry Sheriff, but I can't get you in today. In fact, I'm being sent home in about an hour myself. I'm sorry."

"I understand," Daryl said. "Thanks."

Bradley extended a hand and Daryl shook it.

"Thanks for helping out, Sheriff," Bradley said. "Sorry I can't do more for you."

"No problem," Daryl said. "Let me know the next time you're up this way. I'll buy the drinks."

"You're on," Bradley said.

Daryl watched as Agent Bradley turned and walked to the group of gawkers pressing against the tape and told them to move back.

Daryl sat in his car and watched the scene. He had come out to this part of the country to get away from this kind of circus. He thought about the times he had been in one of those uniforms now giving the orders inside the tape. At first, those times had been interesting, but after a while, they had all begun to smell the same; somebody had wanted something and the way they tried to get it was to screw with someone else's life. He knew that whatever had happened here in Lindell was the same, he just wasn't sure who had done it and what the hell they were wanting to get out of it. And this time, Sheriff Daryl Krebel knew whose lives had been screwed-up in the process. At some point, he had visited with all seventeen of them. Hell, he had eaten in most of their homes. He had come out here because he was sick and tired of this kind of thing and never wanted to deal with it again. As he sat in his car this afternoon, there was a growing feeling in his gut that he was not about to let some ass-holes with yellow tape keep him from finding out who messed with those seventeen people.

Daryl Krebel had no idea what he was going to do, but he was sure as hell going to do it.

Chapter 17

Emily stared at the glass.

She thought about how it was little glasses like this that had caused so much of the trouble over the years. So many arguments. So many broken promises. So many hours spent listening to the foolishness that came out of her parents' mouths because their brains were overloaded with the alcohol from little glasses just like this one. Her mind raced with memories of the times she felt like the only adult in the house, even when she was still in single digits.

That little glass.

She hadn't come to the little bar in Marigny to drink. She usually came here for the music, but it was too early in the day for that. One guy sat on a chair plucking at a guitar, but it would be overly gracious to call what he was doing music. She glanced up from the glass at the two or three people sitting at the bar. Two guys and a woman, all who knew exactly why they had come in here and were following up on that goal. They had given up any hope of pretending the little glass didn't mess things up and just accepted the fact that the best way to forget about the mess was to get more glasses. Emily was grateful that her parents had caught-on before that happened and had at least tried to straighten things out. But she still lived with the little watermark circles all those glasses had left on her mind over the years. It's why she didn't drink much herself. Maybe a beer now and then or maybe a glass of wine, but not the stuff in the little glass on the table. That little glass was the enemy.

But today? Why not just pick up that glass and wash the pains away? Hell, maybe even have a second one. Even this couldn't do much to make this day suck any more than it already did.

Emily took a breath and picked up the little glass.

"Starting kind of early, aren't ya?" the voice said.

Emily shook her head without looking up.

"Look," she said. "I'm not in the mood. Go find another table."

"I don't know, Lance," the voice said. "Do you see another table you like as much as this one?"

Emily looked up to see Colonel Bill Chambers and Commander Lance Reyes.

"What the hell..." Emily said.

"Mind if we sit down?" Chambers said as they dragged chairs to the table.

Emily put the little glass on the table.

"I'm guessing its no accident we have bumped into each other here?" Emily said.

"No," Chamber said. "No accident. We need to talk with you."

"And my guess is it's not to tell me I won the lottery or something?"

"No, sorry," Chamber said.

"Have you heard about what happened in Kansas yesterday?" Lance Reyes said.

"Nothing since last night. It appears I no longer have access to that kind of information."

"We heard about that," Chambers said. "That's part of what we need to talk about too."

"You heard I'm out? News gets around fast."

"Em, this may not make any sense right now," Reyes said, "but the fact that you're out of the agency for a bit may actually be a good thing."

"Define good," Emily said.

"Bill will explain. You going to drink that?" Reyes nodded toward the little glass on the table.

"No," Emily said, "don't think so. Help yourself."

Reyes did.

"Emily, I'll give you the short version now, and if you are willing to help us out we'll fill in the rest. You know the VanHollings group, from the landfill thing?"

"Sure, are they not complying?"

"It looks worse than that. VanHollings is dead, along with Herzig and Geller, maybe more, we're still trying to find out."

"Dead? What..."

"They say a heart attack. But, it looks more like there is some kind of coup in the group. We don't know who is behind it or what they're going to do, things are moving too fast. But that's not all of it."

Chambers looked at Reyes.

"You know that VanHollings had a son, his name is Klass?"

"I guess so, yeah. Is he doing this?"

"VanHollings put his son in charge of one of their projects, like the landfill thing, and it seems that the son decided to go off on his own and create his own little empire. We think they're the ones behind the thing in Kansas."

"Wait," Emily said. "So, the first group, the one we thought we had under control, is going through some kind of, what do we call it, reorganization? And now we also have this Klass kid starting up his own group trying to do things like the first one? Is that what you're saying?"

"Afraid so," Reyes said.

"They're not working together?" Emily said. "So, did the Klass kid kill his own father?"

"Doesn't look like it," Chambers said. "But, what the kid's group is doing will create more problems for the old group than we ever did."

"And we don't know who's taking control of the old group?" Emily said.

"No. But apparently wasn't Herzig or Geller."

"And you have come to ask me to figure it out, is that it?"

"No, not quite," Reyes said. "There's still another piece. That's where you come in."

"How?" Emily said.

"Em, one or both of these groups have help inside."

"Inside? Inside what? The agency?"

"Not just the agency," Chambers said. "We know the first group has been around for years and has gotten a lot of their supporters put in key positions in government, military, the agency, and lots of other places. Those people are well hidden and haven't done anything to risk their jobs, but they help smooth the way for the group to do what they want done."

"Like get you out of the way," Reyes said.

"Me?"

"It wasn't Mercer that got you out, Em," Chambers said. "This has been in the works for months, this came from someplace else. Someplace inside. Someplace high-up."

"And now, having you outside the agency means they have less actual control over you," Reyes said. "So you may be able to help us out. That's why we're here."

Emily looked at the empty glass.

"What's wrong?" Reyes said.

"Inside?" Emily said. "Maybe like a Senator or something like that?"

"Could be," Chambers said. "Why a Senator?"

"Just something Dasilva said on the phone last night," Emily said. "When he called to chew me out. He said he had gotten a lot of calls about me, even one from a Senator. I'm just wondering."

"Did he say which one?" Reyes said.

"No, and I didn't even think anything about it until what you just said about someone on the inside. Do you think you could find out which Senator called him?"

"Probably," Chambers said. "We can try."

"Yeah, do that," Emily said. "I'm curious if...well, just let me know what you find out."

"If what?" Reyes said.

"It's probably nothing, "Emily said. "It's just that I had some, uh, issues with someone a long time ago who is now a Senator, and I'm just wondering. Does Dasilva know about all this? The inside stuff, I mean?"

"Don't think so, but we've not talked with him," Chambers said. "We think he's clean, but we can't take the chance to find out. We don't know who is on what team at this point."

Silence.

"It's just the timing," Emily said.

"What do you mean?" Chambers said.

"It's my dad, he's in pretty bad shape. I just don't know that I can get away right now."

"Hell, Em," Chambers said, "we didn't know your dad was in that shape."

"I just found out an hour or so ago myself."

"Forget it then," Reyes said. "You need to take care of your dad. We'll handle this stuff."

"No," Emily said, "I just don't..."

"I'll tell you what," Chambers said. "We may call if we have a question or two if that's alright. But he's your dad, Em, that's where you belong right now."

"But..."

"No buts," Chambers said. "It's good seeing you Em."

The guitar player was still making noise when she looked up and noticed the blue and red lights reflecting in the empty glass on the table. The third squad car went by as she walked out the door and started down Frenchman Street.

Chapter 18

He walked down Chartres Street and turned South on Barracks. It was a safe area on the Eastern edge of the Quarter, especially in the mid-afternoon. He had just crossed the street near the hotel's gated parking lot when the two men grabbed him. They dragged him between a couple of cars in the narrow alley. One of them pulled a knife. Moments later the two walked back onto Barracks Street, went the half-block to Decatur Street, and became just two more faces in the crowds of the French Market. Two hours later they were on a plane.

The police were already investigating when Emily walked up to the yellow tape that stretched across Barracks Street.

"You bored or something? What brings an FBI agent down here with us common folk?"

Emily smiled at Ramon Manzanares as he walked down the sidewalk. They had both come to the city about the same time, just in other departments, so they occasionally had a drink or a bowl of gumbo and compared stories.

"Just stopped by to see how things are really done, I guess," Emily said.

"Well, come take a look for yourself."

Apparently, word had not gotten around about her change in employment, and after hesitating just long enough to imagine Dasilva yelling at her, she ducked under the tape and followed Manzanares to the alley.

They stayed far enough back to be out of the way of the teams leading the investigation, but Emily could see the body lying in the gravel and weeds. Emily saw the blood and thought it must have been done by someone who knew how to make it quick. One of the investigators examining the body stood up. Emily saw the face lying on the gravel. She heard herself take a gulp of air.

"What's wrong?" Manzanares said?

"Do you have any identification of the victim?" Emily said.

"No, he was clean. Why, do you know him?"

"No," Emily said. "I don't really know him. I just met him a time or two."

Emily paused.

"His name was Steve."

Chapter 19

"Hey, I sure thought it was going to take longer than this. We're there already!"

"We're still in Missouri, doofus. You do realize there is more than one Springfield don't you?"

"I know that. Geez, I was just messin' with you. You need to relax a bit," Danny Whitley said.

Traffic was light as the truck followed I-44 around the North side of Springfield, Missouri.

"Relax? I'll relax when we get up there and get done. That thing in the back just gives me the creeps."

"You don't have to worry about the device," Danny said. "It is perfectly harmless until I activate it, and I'm not doing that until everything is ready."

"Ok, but I'll still feel better when we're away from it. Hey, did you see that sign? It said something about the home of Nathan Boone. Was that Daniel Boone? Did they call him that?"

"Nah, he was one of Daniel Boone's sons. I think he fought in the War of 1812 or something like that."

"So he was a soldier, like us."

"Yeah, I guess so," Danny said. "Except he went around on horseback with guns and swords and stuff, and we're driving down the road with a EMP in the back. But other than that, yeah, like us."

"I mean he fought to defend his country, just like we're fighting to defend ours. That's what I meant."

"Yeah, but we're not just defending it, we're going to turn it into what it was meant to be in the first place, what the Bible says it ought to be. He was a solder, but we are God's Soldiers. That makes us different."

"And it means there is no way we can lose!"

"Absolutely!"

Chapter 20

Emily watched the tourists as she walked down Bourbon Street. She never came down here with the crowds and their fancy drinks, but she needed something to distract her from the past two hours with the investigators and all their questions. And then someone learned about her layoff and raised hell about her being inside the yellow tape in the first place.

"Hey, I bet I know where you got those shoes," he said.

Emily reached for her badge to flash it and was immediately reminded of her morning. That made her even more angry, so she stopped. She never stopped to deal with these buskers and their stupid games. They came up and said something like "I bet I know where you got those shoes!" or "I bet I know how many kids your parents had!" Of course, you had your shoes on your feet and your parents had all of their kids, but if you said anything to them, or engaged with them in any way at all, you were playing the game. And if you played their game, you had to pay them. If you engaged with them but did not pay, some of them got down-right nasty about it. So she never stopped. Until today. She stopped and looked directly into the glassy eyes of the young man standing in front of her.

"I bet I know how far I can kick your balls down this street."

For a second, Emily felt just as surprised as the look on the guy's face. He slowly turned and walked away, and she looked at her reflection in a shop window.

"Girl," she said, "you need to do something about all this before you do something really stupid."

It was then she saw the sign in the window. Maybe it had been unconscious, but she was now standing right in front of the VooDoo shop owned by Angelique Fanchon Decourdreau. She walked through the open door and Angelique was waiting.

"Miss Em, I've been expecting you."

Emily felt the vibration and pulled out her phone.

"Graham!"

"Emily, this is Linda. I wanted you to know we had to take your dad to the hospital. I'm afraid he's having some real problems. I've been trying to reach you. I thought you would want to know."

"My phone was off for a while while I dealt with the police. How long have you…never mind. I'm on my way."

Angelique nodded and handed Emily a small cloth bag.

"You go," Angelique said. "I will be here."

Chapter 21

Emily stepped from the elevator and walked to the cardiac wing. Nurse Linda Despre was standing outside a door.

"Linda, what are you doing here?"

"My shift was about over," Linda said, "and he just seemed so confused I thought it might help calm him down if I came along for a while."

Emily paused.

"I can't tell you how much I appreciate that, Linda. All that you've done. I really..."

"I'm happy to be here. He's a special kind of guy. The doctor is with him now. I think they're just finishing up."

The door opened and a young man came out.

"Are you here with Mr. Graham?" the doctor said.

"I am, yes, I'm his daughter, Emily. How is he?"

"We are doing everything we can at this point. His blood pressure isn't responding the way we would like it too, and he has some irregularity in his heart. Is that normal for him?"

"Not that I know of," Emily said as she looked at Linda. "This is his nurse from Torchwood. She may know more than I do."

"No, he has no history of irregularities," Linda said. "But today has been pretty stressful for him."

"How long has he been experiencing the dementia episodes?" the doctor said.

"Oh, about two or three years now," Emily said, "but not all the time."

"I see," the doctor said. "That is a long time for this type of dementia. Unfortunately, it takes a real toll on the body and can impact a patient's life expectancy. And after this long, well, we will do what we can. You can go in if you would like."

"Thank you, doctor," Emily said.

"You go ahead," Linda said. "I need to call my family and let them know where I am."

Dad was lying in bed with one arm stretched out toward the wall and was slowly opening and closing his fingers. A nurse was checking the IV tubes.

"I'm Emily, his daughter," Emily said, "how is he doing?"

"He's resting right now, which is good," the nurse said. "I'm not sure what he is doing with his hand. He doesn't appear to be in any pain."

Emily moved to the side of the bed. She noticed his lips moving but couldn't make out what he was saying. She leaned closer.

"My god," Emily said.

"What's wrong?" the nurse said.

"He is talking to his dogs," Emily said. "That's what he is doing with his hand. He's petting his dogs. He is talking to each one of them, telling them goodbye."

Emily had a hard time finding breath. The room was getting blurry. She cleared her throat to regain composure.

"Well, hi kiddo, it's good to see you," Dad said as he looked up.

"Hi Dad, how you feeling?"

"Just a bit tired. I think I'll take a short nap, and in the morning we can talk about what you're going to do about Rebecca. Nite babe."

He closed his eyes.

"Nite Dad," Emily said.

"It's the medication," the nurse said. "It's going to make him drowsy. He needs his rest."

Emily nodded and started to the door to talk with Linda. She heard him take a deep breath and turned to look. The nurse was leaning over the bed. Then she raised her eyes to meet Emily's.

"He's gone," the nurse said.

Chapter 22

Several things had to have happened, but the next thing Emily remembered was standing on the steps across from Jackson Square, looking at the river. A young man with glassy eyes was walking towards her. The young man did not say anything about shoes or about parents, but just held a small piece of paper out in his hand.

Emily took a breath.

"What's this?" Emily said, "another game?"

"They paid me to give it to you," he said, "that's all I know. So here."

Emily took the paper and watched the young man stumble up the stairs. She wiped the mist from her eyes, opened the paper and read it. All she saw was the name of a familiar little place just a block or so away. Emily looked at the note and then at the river. The water flowed by in the darkness just like it did every night.

"What next?" she said. She violated her number one rule by speaking those words, but at this point, she couldn't imagine how the night could get any worse. She crossed Jackson square, found the little bar, and forced her feet to walk inside.

The waitress stopped and Emily ordered water because it was the only thing that didn't require her to make any kind of decision. The waitress smiled, kind of, and brought the glass.

"I am so glad you came," the voice said. "May I join you?"

The woman was older, dressed more for one of the upscale French Quarter places than for this dive.

Emily nodded, and the woman sat in the chair next to her.

"I appreciate you being willing to…"

"Look," Emily said. "I don't mean to be rude, and you look like a nice enough person, but I've had one hell of a day and I'm really not in the mood for conversation, or a sales pitch, or much of anything else right now. So, please, pardon my bluntness, but who are you and what do you want?"

"I understand. My name is Adriana. Adriana VanHollings. I believe you knew my husband."

Emily had a gifted imagination. For just a second, she had the vision of an elephant dressed in bluejeans and a sparkling Elvis jacket and being ridden by three piano playing monkeys walk into the cafe and order a beignet. And nothing, not even that elephant, would have surprised her as much as what she had just heard. It was just a quick thought in her imagination. But very clear.

"You are smiling," Adriana VanHollings said. "Did I say something amusing?"

"No," Emily said. "You just surprised me a bit, that's all. What can I do for you Mrs. VanHollings? Oh, and I was sorry to hear the news about your husband."

"Call me Adriana, please. And yes, thank you. I'll be blunt. I want to talk with you about what we might do for each other; about an opportunity that could be of benefit to both of us."

Emily was silent.

"Emily, I need your help. That's what I've come to talk with you about. I have a problem that needs someone with your abilities to address."

"My abilities?"

"Emily, anyone who could handle my dear, late husband the way you did is exactly the person I need. By the way, he told me what you said to him that day at the beach. 'You are blocking my light!' Honestly, I thought it was priceless. So, what do you think? You are now in the perfect situation to be able to help me. Will you do that?"

"You haven't said what it is that you want me to do," Emily said.

"Yes, well, I can usually take care of things myself without any outside help, but this time, well, it is different. It is personal. It has to do with my son."

"Your son?" Emily said.

"His name is Klass, and I'm afraid he has become somewhat of a family rebel. He and his father always fought about everything. They were too much alike. Berend wanted Klass to one day take over the business but he insisted that it be done his way. Klass wanted to be his own man, if you know what I mean. Berend put Klass in charge of one of the group's projects hoping it might help him mature and behave, but I'm afraid it didn't work out. Klass has taken that project and turned it into something of his own, something he was going to use to show his father up."

"So what is it that you want me to do?" Emily said.

"Klass and his group must be stopped," Adriana VanHollings said. "It is going to be difficult. Klass has help from many people in very powerful roles. Some of them are in business, some in politics, some may even be in your agency."

"Powerful roles," Emily said. "Maybe someone like a Senator?"

Adrianna's pupils narrowed slightly.

"Senator?" Adrianna said. Why a Senator?"

"Oh, you just mentioned politics and it was the first thing that popped into my head, that's all."

"I really wouldn't have any idea who or where they are, but Klass has told me they exist. And one other thing; they need to be stopped, but I do not want Klass harmed. Even with all this, he is my son. His behavior is more my husband's fault than his own."

"I understand," Emily said. "What are you looking at?"

"Oh, I'm sorry," Adrianna said. "That bracelet on your wrist. It is beautiful. Where ever did you find it?"

"This?" Emily said as she touched the bracelet. "It was a gift from a friend. Someone I worked with. I'm not sure where she got it."

"It is really wonderful," Adrianna said, "I am going to have to look for one like it. I am sorry, but I tend to notice things like that. What were we talking about?"

"A while ago you said something about me being in a perfect situation. Just what situation is that?"

"Well, being put out of the agency like you were. I know it is frustrating. However, you may actually have more power now that you are outside of the agency. You have all of the knowledge and insights, and I'm sure you still have the connections. But now you are no longer limited by their control. Emily, this may actually be a great opportunity for you."

"I just want to know who did it," Emily said. "I want to know who was behind it."

"Emily, don't you see, it doesn't matter who did it. What matters is that now you are in a position to do things you never could have done before. And, Emily, we can give you whatever you need to do the job, and have anything you ever want. You could have never done that on the inside, surely you see that."

Emily's face gave away her reaction.

"Emily, do you see the man sitting on the stool over there at the bar? The one on the end with the jacket on?"

"What about him?"

"His name is Raul. He works for me. For the group. Right now he is here to make sure I am safe and that no one interferes with

58

anything I am doing. If you work with us he will do that for you as well. He and many others."

Emily glanced at Raul.

"Emily, I need you to help with Klass, but that's just the beginning. We are changing everything about how our group does business. The things my husband did are outdated. They are the ideas of old men and simply cannot work today. We are changing that, and you can be a part of that change. This is the beginning of something truly amazing, Emily, and I want you to be a part of it."

Emily looked at her water glass.

"Please, just think about it. You've had a very difficult day today, but they could be the last difficulties you ever have to face. We need you Emily, and I believe you need us. Think about it. Here is my number. Give me a call tomorrow and we will get started."

Adriana VanHollings stood. Raul moved from the barstool and walked toward the door. She stopped and walked back to the table.

"And Emily, I forgot to say how sorry I was to hear about your father. We will all have you in our thoughts."

"How did you know about that?" Emily said. "It just happened."

"Emily, we make it a habit to keep an eye on our friends. It is how we all take care of each other."

Thirty minutes later, Emily sat in the darkness of her bedroom and stared in the direction of the ceiling. At some point, she closed her eyes and was on the beach. Her dad's casket was surrounded by flowers and the crowd erupted as Jimmy Buffett walked onto the stage to sing the eulogy. The beach was filled with Parrothead Buffet fans and it seemed like most of them stood between Emily and the stage. She tried to move closer. The person in front of her turned around and laughed. It was Adriana VanHollings. Berend VanHollings was with her. In front of them was that crazy doctor from the towboat, and that landfill hacker and his boss, Typhos. Dasilva was there. They were all in front of her, keeping her from getting closer to the stage, Jimmy Buffett, and her dad. And they were all laughing at her. And up there, right next to the stage, she saw fourth-grade Rebecca. Rebecca looked at Emily.

"He's gone," Rebecca said with a grin.

Emily was shaking as she paced the floor trying to get the dream out of her head, but it had helped her make her decision. She reached for her phone and punched in the number.

"Hello?"

"Noon tomorrow," Emily said. "Same place as today."

Chapter 23

"Hey, wake up!" Danny Whitley said. "We need to get going."

The two men opened the doors of the semi-trailer and pulled out the ramps. Danny climbed up into the trailer and seconds later backed the delivery truck down the ramps into the warehouse.

"Get in," Danny said. "I'll drive from here."

"We're just leaving the semi?"

"It's done its job. Let's go."

They pulled into traffic on I-270 and headed East. No one paid any attention to the two men in the parcel delivery truck as it turned North on I-55 toward Springfield, Illinois.

Chapter 24

"It wasn't your fault, Ronnie. We all agreed it was the right thing to do."

"I know, but I should have replaced him sooner. This was his last activity. He was just going there to introduce her to her new connection. I had no idea things had gone this far."

"None of us did," Grandpa said. "I mean, we knew something was going on with Graham, but-"

"I should have..."

"Ronnie, you can't do that. We do the best we think we can do. That's all we can do. We learn from our decisions, but we can't second-guess them. And even though we don't like using connections more than one time, we all agreed it was the thing to do this time."

"I know. It's just that-"

"What we need to focus on right now is why this happened," Grandpa said. "Why did someone take out one of our connections? Was it just a random attack, or did they know what he was doing? And more importantly, do they know who he was doing it for? Are we at risk of being revealed? We cannot allow that to happen."

"I understand."

Ronnie looked out the window as he drank from his coffee.

"Look," Grandpa said, "we will find out what is going on and we will deal with it. We have been in far more difficult situations in the past, believe me. We just need to stay focused. What do we know so far?"

"He was grabbed by two guys in the middle of the day. Pretty bold. They knew what they were doing."

"That probably rules out a simple robbery or mugging then," Grandpa said.

"Yeah, and the two weren't local. We've been able to trace them back to the airport where they caught a flight to Tulsa about two hours after the hit. It looks like they flew in from there earlier yesterday morning."

"And when they got back to Tulsa?" Grandpa said.

"They knew how to lose a tail."

"We don't know where they went?" Grandpa said.

"That's where it gets interesting. We don't have anything from the usual sources with the cameras and plate scanners. But, we have another source telling us they left Tulsa heading East. A source that has access to satellite data."

"Satellite?" Grandpa said. "You mean military?"

"Not formal military, no," Ronnie said. "That's the interesting part. We've tried getting help from our usual government sources but they haven't been very helpful. What we're getting is coming from…"

"Wait," Grandpa said. "What do you mean they haven't been very helpful?"

"Well, it's just taking a lot longer than usual to get anything from them. And in some cases, they say they don't have the information we're looking for, even though it's stuff they have always had before."

"Sounds to me like someone is holding out," Grandpa said. "Like there might be some people who don't want us to have the information we need? Sounds like there are some people inside playing for the other team, don't ya' think? So, who is this other source then if they're not military?"

"I don't know that yet," Ronnie said.

They drank from their coffee.

"So," Grandpa said, "let me see if I'm understanding what we're dealing with here. We have the old VanHollings' group going through some kind of bloody, internal battle for control. We have VanHollings' son creating his own new group to try and show up his father's. We have somebody, maybe one of those two groups, using some kind of electronic bomb to do something we're not clear about yet. We have two guys, maybe from one of those groups, identifying and killing one of our connections. We have one of our long-term sources suddenly decide to begin holding out information from us. And we have some other maybe-military group providing us with that missing information. Is that about it?"

"And Graham," Ronnie said.

"Oh, yes, and we have one of our people suddenly booted from her job because of pressure from inside the agency, or maybe from even higher than that. Now, do I have it?"

"Yeah, I think so."

Ronnie looked out the window..

"Grandpa," Ronnie said. "I need to ask you a question. It's about Agent Graham. How did she get so involved in all of this? I mean, with everything she's done. How did she get into this in the first place?"

Grandpa drank the last of his coffee.

"Maybe we can talk about that tomorrow," Grandpa said as he stood. "I need to think. I'm going fishing."

Ronnie watched as the older man walked out the door and down the sidewalk.

Chapter 25

"Good morning, Ms. Graham. Or shall I call you Emily? My name is Franklin."

He had a black suit, black shoes, clean-cut hair, eyes like a Labrador Retriever, a deep voice that oozed of sympathy, and an overall look that Emily thought he must have practiced for hours in front of a mirror as part of a class at undertaker school.

"Emily is fine," she said. "I appreciate your seeing me so early this morning."

"No problem at all," Franklin said. "We're happy to do whatever we can do to help. You said in your call that you wanted something very simple for your father?"

"Yes. He made it very clear he did not want anything formal. No service, no visitation, no flowers. He just wanted to be cremated and that's it."

"I see. We can certainly help with that."

Pause.

"But, let me say this. We certainly want to honor your father's wishes, but we also know that it is very important that we do what we can to help you through this difficult time. Sometimes having even just a simple ceremony, even with just a few close friends, can..."

"I appreciate that, but you did not know my father. He was a captain on the river, and one of his favorite sayings was 'I am a Captain, I have been a Captain for forty-five years, and I will be a Captain for ten years after I'm dead and gone!' He was very clear about what he wanted, and if I do anything to change that, well, let's just stick with his plan, okay?"

"Of course. I understand. I will make the arrangements. When would you like to do this?"

"Do what?"

"Well, many families want to have a brief get-together before the cremation, a time of remembrance, something like that. It is a time when they-"

"No, he didn't want anything like that, anything at all. Just the cremation is all."

"That's fine, it looks like we can do that tomorrow afternoon if that is alright with you."

"Sure, I appreciate it."

"Would you like to select an urn now? We have a nice selection of…"

"He just wanted a cardboard box. Do you have that?"

"Cardboard? Well, we do have what we call a scattering tube. It's made of something like cardboard and is meant as a temporary container for those intended to do something else with the remains. We also have…"

"That will work," Emily said. "Let's do that."

"Very good. I will get this all taken care of and call you to let you know when you can come and get the remains. Would you like to see him?"

Emily sat up in her chair as the room began spinning.

"What?"

"Would you like to have a moment with your father? We dressed him in the clothes you sent over, and I thought you might want to see him before we do the cremation. He is in the next room."

Emily glanced at the door Franklin pointed to, and the years came crashing back in one rush. The good. The not-so-good. The wonderful. The horrendous. She had felt something similar at her mother's visitation five years ago, but this was more. Bigger. With all of the ups and downs and craziness, this was daddy behind that door. Emily mumbled something as Franklin opened the door and she stepped into the small room.

Chapter 26

The delivery truck turned South on Second Street and drove the five blocks to East Capital Avenue. They turned left onto East Capital and then into the parking lot just before the railroad tracks. They parked in the space between the two large buildings and turned on the truck's flashers. No one ever questioned a delivery truck parked with its flashers on. Danny Whitley stepped into the back of the van, and then he and his partner stepped from the truck and walked between the two buildings toward Second Street. They walked two blocks to the parking lot where the car was waiting. Danny looked at the driver.

"I didn't expect to see you here!" Danny said.

"I go where God tells me to go," Klass VanHollings said. "Is everything ready?"

"Everything is fine," Danny said.

"How long?"

"About eleven minutes," Danny said as Klass turned the car onto Sixth Street toward the airport and the private plane.

"Praise the Lord!" Klass VanHollings said.

Klass parked in the airport rental car lot, got out, and stood facing downtown. Klass raised his arms up over his head and held them there.

"What's that about?" Danny said.

"Exodus seventeen," Klass said. "Let the war begin."

Chapter 27

"You're Charlie's girl, aren't you?"

She was in a wheelchair outside Torchwood's front door, holding an upside-down magazine in one hand and an unlit cigarette in the other.

"Yes, I am," Emily said.

"I was sorry to hear the news this morning. He was ornery, but he always made me laugh. I'm going to miss him."

"Me too, thanks," Emily said.

He slid his walker in front of Emily as she passed the dining room.

"I was sorry to hear about your dad," he said.

"Thank you."

"You're the one who brought him all the ice cream?"

"Yeah, that was me."

"We had a hell of a time with that, I'll tell you. We sat there telling stories, most of them lies."

"Yeah, he was good at that."

"He was a good man," he said. "It's a damn shame."

"Yes," Emily said. "Thanks."

There were three or four more conversations before she got to the room. There was no one at the nurse's station so Emily went into the room to begin collecting his things. There was a large plastic bag on the bed.

"I put everything in that sack for you," Linda said from the doorway behind her. "I hope you don't mind."

Emily smiled.

"No, thanks Linda," Emily said. "And thanks for being there last night. It meant a lot, and I know it meant a lot to dad. Even if he couldn't say it."

"I'm going to miss him," Linda said. "Who am I going to argue with now?"

A bell rang at the nurse's station.

"I need to get that," Linda said. "You might take one more look around and make sure I didn't miss anything. Especially those shoes of his. I don't want him to come back and haunt me because of those shoes."

"And he could probably do that, too," Emily said. "Thanks, I'll take a look."

She didn't hear him come in the room.

"Emily?"

He looked younger than the others.

"Yes?"

"I was sorry to hear about your father," he said.

"Thank you. Were you one of his ice cream buddies?" Emily said as she opened a drawer.

"No," he said as he moved closer, "I'm not a resident here. In fact, I'm not here now."

Emily stopped and looked up.

"Not here? Wait. Who are you?"

"My name is Steve," he said. "Yes, it's quite a coincidence, I know, but I am a connection like the other Steve was," he said.

"What happened to him, to Steve? Do you know?"

"We don't know much more than you do right now, but we will find out and I will tell you what I am able to tell you. But there are other things you need to know right now."

"What things?"

"Berend VanHollings. It was not a heart attack. And Herzig, Geller, and Conway were not by chance either. You need to-"

"Are we interrupting anything?" the large, line-backer-sized security guard said as the two entered the room. "We heard you were here and just had to come down to say how sorry we are about the Captain."

"Oh, yes, thank you," Emily said. "Well, we were just talking here and..." Emily looked around and realized that she and the two guards were the only ones in the room.

"Uh, yeah, thank you. I appreciate what you did for dad, and I'm just sorry for the trouble he caused you."

"He was no trouble at all, though I wouldn't have told him that. He just kept us on our toes. I think he kind of enjoyed doing that."

"Yes, he liked stirring things up, that's for sure."

"Well, we won't keep you," the tall guard said. "We just wanted to let you know how sorry we are. If there is anything we can do-"

"Thank you. I really do appreciate that. And thanks again for taking care of him."

She was alone in the room with the plastic bag, her memories, and a growing list of questions.

.

Chapter 28

Larry Renshaw was in the basement of the East Cook Street communications station, thirteen-hundred feet from the truck. The building was built to hold the massive equipment that used to manage the large microwave cones sitting on top of the building's tower. Now the tower holds the cell phone and emergency systems relay equipment and the box-like microwave dishes are empty shells. The basement was originally designed to survive a nuclear attack and hold enough supplies for several hundred people to live for six months. Now it was lined with fiber cables leading to a collection of server rooms like the one Larry was working in. Larry had just opened the door of a server cabinet when the room lights flickered. As he turned, the room lights dimmed. He heard ventilation fans slow down. Some of his servers shut-down. Alarms began to flash and shout. He looked around the room and saw some servers down while others appeared to be running normally. He reached for his phone to call upstairs to see if they knew what was going on. His phone had no signal. He heard shouting from another room down the hall. His mind raced as more alarms began, more servers went down, the ventilation fans stopped, and the lights grew darker.

Chuck Donahue was putting a customer's package on the scale at his window of the United States Post Office, nine hundred feet from the truck. He glanced at the clock to see if the morning was really moving as slowly as it seemed to be. The digital scale began to show the numbers when the little screen went dark. Chuck looked up and then noticed that the lights in the building were off. The customers in line were either looking at a dead phone, tablet, or laptop, at the darkness of the now unlit spaces behind the counter or out the window at what was happening there. Chuck wondered why the power would go off like this and the emergency lighting and other backup things had not kicked in.

Kinsey Elliott was standing outside Senate committee hearing room on the fourth floor of the State Capital Building, eight hundred feet from the truck. She was doing her best to convince a Senator to see her side of the bill about to be brought before the committee. The conversation had not been going well. Her first thought was that the senator had hung-up on her. Her second thought was that she had forgotten to recharge her phone, and now the Senator would probably think she had hung up on him. Then she realized the hallway had gotten darker, and quieter. Doors opened as people stepped from dark offices.

Walter Beaton was at his desk in the Attorney General's Office, two-hundred-thirty feet South of the truck. He was reviewing the notes from an interview he had conducted yesterday. He noticed the lights in the room grow brighter for a moment and then go out. His computer screen went black. He thought of the deadline for completing his report and glanced at his watch. It was dead. The battery-powered desk clock his wife had given him for his birthday had stopped.

Denosha Morgan was driving the ambulance up Second Street with the elderly victim of what appeared to be a heart attack. The lights and siren helped clear traffic as she passed East Jackson Street, two hundred feet West of the truck. She had just slowed to go around another car when her siren stopped. Suddenly, she had a hard time steering and had to pull hard to straighten the ambulance out again. The engine had stopped, along with the siren, lights, and power steering. Denosha tried to restart the engine but nothing happened, not even that click she hears when the battery is down. Nothing happened. Nothing at all. Her partner in the back yelled that her equipment had all just crashed. Denosha grabbed the radio to get help but it was not working. She glanced out the window at the other cars stopped in the streets as she climbed into the back of the dark ambulance to help with the CPR.

Lanna Gilbert had just pressed the elevator button for the second floor Appellate Courtroom, seventy feet North of the truck. She had come in a half-hour early to make sure she was on time for her meeting with the judge. The elevator began to move as Lanna opened her folder to make sure she had everything she needed. Then the elevator stopped. Her first thought was about the other times this had happened, and that it would only be a minute or two before it would

71

move again. But it had never been this dark. And never this quiet. She felt for the buttons but none of them did anything. She found and pressed the emergency bell but nothing happened. She picked up the emergency phone. It was dead. In the quietness, she could hear people on the floors below and above her. Lanna shouted to let someone know where she was.

Kyle Bagshaw sat on the barstool he sat on every morning watching his drink quiver as another train passed by the window, eleven hundred feet from the truck. He didn't notice the darkness of the room or even the dark television and silent jukebox. He didn't wear a watch or carry a phone, and he didn't ever pay attention to what other people were saying, even if they shouted. What he watched was the train and the puffs of smoke coming from the wheels as they locked and tried to drag the freight to a stop. This was new.

The area around the Illinois State Capital Complex is the home of a number of government departments and agencies, as well as a long list of groups who do business with them. It is usually a busy and noisy place. This morning, the streets around the complex were cluttered with stopped vehicles. Traffic lights were dark, as were all other lights that spoke of companies, restaurants, and advertisements. Crowds stood around some buildings trying to help others get in or out of unresponsive automatic doors. The normal hum from massive air conditioning units and other machinery was replaced by silence. Government business, and any other business usually completed in a normal morning around the complex, was not completed this morning.

It was like someone had pulled the plug.

Chapter 29

"You're sure about this?"

"Yeah, I'm sure," Emily said.

The same three drinkers were at the bar, and Emily was at the corner table with Bill Chambers, Lance Reyes, and her bottle of water.

"I just thought," Chambers said, "because of your dad and all. We could wait a few…"

"Thanks, but no, I'm going to do this!"

"You realize," Reyes said, "if you do, people inside the agency will find out. And that means some of those people may do their best to see to it that you never get back in there again."

"Yeah, I know."

"We just want to make sure you…"

"Look, guys, I appreciate your worrying about me and all. But, to tell you the truth, I don't think I could go back even if that was possible. This isn't the first time I've…I mean, I know what's going on there. Not all of it, but I know enough to realize that most of the things that made me want to be in the agency in the first place are gone. They've taken that away from me, and it pisses me off. It's Rebecca all over again."

"Who's Rebecca?" Reyes said.

"Oh, never mind. It's just that I sat there yesterday watching dad sleep. He worked hard his entire life, you know, and he ended up laying there stressing out about his damn shoes and talking to his dead dogs. And the thing is, he did it to himself. He's the one who made the decisions that got him there. Some of the things the boat companies did to him were plain rotten, but he put up with it. For us, his family. He just let them do those things so he could keep his job. He was a good, company man, and look where it got him. And then I woke up last night thinking about everything that's going on, and why it's going on, and I realized I had some decisions to make. For me."

Emily drank from her water.

"I could sit here and just let things happen while I do whatever it is everyone thinks I ought to be doing after dad died. Or, I could call VanHollings back and do the things she wants me to do until she decides to have someone take care of me like she did her husband and the others. I could just sit here and let..."

She took another drink.

"Or, I could go out there and find out what the hell is going on and who's doing it and, damn, I don't know, try and stop them. I may not be able to do it, but at least it's my decision and I'll sleep better at night."

"Wait," Reyes said. "You said Mrs. Vanhollings took care of her husband. What do you mean?"

"It wasn't a heart attack," Emily said. "I don't know for sure, but my guess is that she was involved somehow."

"How do you know it wasn't his heart?" Chambers said.

"Steve told me."

"Steve?" Chambers said. "You talked with him before he was killed?"

"No," Emily said. "It's the new Steve, the second one."

They heard the buzz and Chambers reached for his phone.

"The second one?" Reyes said. "What do you..."

"Shit!" Chambers said.

"What's wrong?" Reyes said just before he heard his own phone.

Emily watched both men's faces until they ended their calls.

"What's wrong?" Emily said.

"There's been a second attack," Chambers said. "In Illinois."

"Illinois?" Emily said. "Where?"

"Springfield," Reyes said as he stood. "It looks like some kind of attack near the Capital complex. You know where that is?"

"Yeah, I know."

"That's right," Chambers said. "You're from up that way, aren't you?"

"We need to go check-in," Reyes said as he pushed back from the table. "You coming with us?"

Emily looked out the window, then stood up.

"No," Emily said. "I've got something I need to do. I'll check in with you later."

Emily followed them out the door and walked down the street to her car. An hour later she stopped at a gas station in Amite City to fill the tank and get some coffee. It was another eleven hours to Springfield.

Chapter 30

Larry Renshaw walked along the row of cabinets trying to make sense of what was happening. He noticed that the servers that had crashed were on the same lines, so he figured the problem must be in one general area. He heard one of the backup generators kicking in from the other side of the basement. The room lights began to brighten as one of the other technicians came to the door.

"Larry, you need to come upstairs and see this!" the tech said.

Chuck Donahue followed protocols and had escorted the customers out of the post office and locked the doors. That was the only piece of the protocol that seemed to work. He had no way to communicate and notify anyone of the situation. He had no way to back up the computer data. After a few minutes, Chuck just stood at the front window and watched what was happening outside.

Kinsey Elliott followed the instructions of the security people clearing the capitol building. As she stood with the group in the yard, she looked around and tried to make sense of what was happening around her.

Walter Beaton put his written notes in his briefcase and followed the usual evacuation procedures. He picked up his laptop and was surprised at how hot it felt. He wondered if somehow his laptop had shorted out and cause whatever it was that had happened. He thought about the paperwork that would be involved in clearing that mess up.

Denosha Morgan opened the rear ambulance door for ventilation and looked around. Looking up Second Street to the North she could see traffic lights working five or six blocks away. She told her partner to continue the CPR and started running North hoping to find a cell phone signal so she could get some help. Either that or she would run all the way to the hospital and get another ambulance herself. If any of them were running.

Lanna Gilbert closed her eyes and imagined the sound of wind in the Aspen trees in the mountains. Someone had heard her shouts and told her they would get help, but right now she was still inside the elevator. And she knew it was just her imagination, but it felt like the elevator was getting smaller. Damned claustrophobia. She had only taken the elevator this morning because of the meeting with the judge. She usually took the stairs. Sometimes even the narrow stairways felt too small, but she could at least keep moving there. Now, she tried to hear the sounds of the stream that ran through the Aspens, as she sat down in a corner of the dark box.

Kyle Bagshaw took another drink from his beer as he looked out the window at the train. He wasn't any expert on railroads, but someone had once told him about the sensors along the rails that would stop the trains if there was some kind of a break or problem with the tracks. He shook his head and took the last drink from his glass. He turned to order a refill, but the bartender had apparently gone somewhere for something. Kyle still hadn't noticed how dark and quiet it had become.

A few people had been able to restart their vehicles and were now threading the maze of stopped traffic. It was made more difficult as the people evacuating buildings flowed from the sidewalks to the streets. Sirens could be heard from the first responders coming to help. Below them, another entire collection of people sat in the darkness of the tunnel hallways that connected the buildings of the capitol complex and reached another mile to the North.

It was even more quiet there.

Chapter 31

Klass watched out the window as the jet climbed to altitude. He smiled.

"Total flight time will be less than an hour, sir," the man standing in the doorway said.

"Thank you," Klass nodded.

"Is there anything you need, sir," the man said. "Anything you need right now?"

"No," Klass said. "I'm fine. Just fine, thank you."

As the man walked back through the doorway, Klass picked up his phone and entered the numbers.

"Senator Murena's office," the voice said. "How may I direct your call?"

"I would like to speak with the Senator please."

"And who may I say is calling?"

"Tell him it's Klass, he'll know."

"One moment please."

Klass watched the pattern of Midwestern agriculture pass below his window. He smiled again.

"I am sorry sir," the voice said. "But the Senator is unavailable right now. May I take a message?"

Klass's smile grew.

"Yes you can, thank you. Please tell the Senator that I will call him again tomorrow morning and that he will want to make sure that he is available to take that call."

"I am sorry, but tomorrow morning the Senator will…"

"And you might tell him that I am calling this time from Springfield. He will understand."

"Um, yes sir, I will give the Senator that message."

Klass put his phone on the table and opened his Bible to Exodus seventeen.

He read for a few moments, then turned to look out the window again. He smiled.

Chapter 32

Daryl hadn't slept well. He had gotten up before dawn and started driving around. He had driven down most every road in his jurisdiction but hadn't spent much of that time thinking and watching as a Sheriff would think and watch. He thought about Lindell and the assholes in the trailers and their damned yellow tape. Of course, they needed to come in and be involved, but they didn't have to pretend they were the only ones who knew anything.

Daryl came to an intersection and turned South.

He had put up with this crap in the service. If it wasn't somebody throwing rank around, it was some politician or corporate jerk-off prancing in thinking they were hot stuff. And even if you knew what was going on a thousand time better than they did, you never had a choice about it; you always had to smile, step out of the way and let the assholes be assholes. And assholes were right up there with the crooks and liars that led him to middle-of-nowhere Lindell. And then they show up here.

"Shit!" Daryl said as he turned West.

He pulled in to the cafe outside Sedan and went inside. The usual crowd was there, like any other morning.

"Well, look what the cat drug in," Suzie said. "What brings you out here this time of the morning darlin'?"

Suzie Pruett owned the place and stood behind the counter the entire day, refilling coffee cups and sassing back at the guys who constantly complained about her food, but came back to eat it every day of the week. Daryl noticed the group of guys was quiet this morning, watching the old television on the wall.

"Hey sunshine," Daryl said. "How about a coffee to go. Black."

Daryl nodded toward the group.

"What's with them?" he said, "Cartoons on this early?"

"No," Suzie said as she poured the coffee. "It's the news. There's been some kind of attack. Some kind of electrical thing. Didn't you hear about it?"

Daryl looked at Suzie.

"Attack? Where?"

"Someplace in Illinois, I think. Springfield, maybe?"

Daryl walked over and stood behind the others watching the screen. A few seconds later he turned and walked to the door.

"Hey," Suzie shouted. "You forgot your coffee!"

Daryl drove home, parked the patrol car by the curb, and tossed the keys on the seat before locking the door. He went inside and threw some clothes in his old duffel bag, and tossed it in his truck. He drove to the gas station, pulled up to a pump, and started filling the tank. He reached in the window, grabbed a map, and opened it on the hood of the truck. He ran his finger along some of the roads, then he folded up the map, tossed it back in the truck, and stood staring in the general direction of Lindell. The gas pump clicked off. Daryl put the pump handle in its slot and closed the gas cap. He reached for his phone, typed a quick text message, and got in his truck.

By the time the County Clerk read Daryl's resignation message, the former Sheriff was already turning his truck onto I-44 heading for Illinois.

Chapter 33

"Adrianna," the Senator said into his phone, "what the hell is going on with your son? Has he gone completely insane?"

"Arthur, I'm afraid I have no idea what you are talking about. What about Klass?"

"What about him? Look at the news. Your son and his little group of lunatics have just done what he's talked about doing for the past three years and started their insane holy war. My God Adrianna, do you realize what this is going to do? The problems it's going to create for the rest of us?"

"Now Arthur, calm down. I don't know what is happening, but I'm sure it's not as bad as you make it sound. And even if there was some kind of attack, why in the world would you think that Klass is involved in it?"

"Because he called me."

"He..."

"Because he called me from where the attack took place so I would know it was him. And because it was the kind of attack he's been talking about, that electronic weapon thing he said he's been working on for the past three years. And don't tell me to calm down. Turn on your television and see how calm you stay."

"I just turned it on. Where was this, this attack?"

"Illinois, the state capital in Springfield. And that's where he called me from, right after it happened."

Silence.

"Adrianna, are you still there?"

Silence.

"Adrianna?"

"I'm here," she said in a different voice than before. "You're sure he was in Springfield when he called you?"

"I had it traced. It came from the phone in his jet, near the Springfield airport."

Silence.

"Adrianna," the Senator said, "you realize what this means, don't you?"

Silence.

"They have to be stopped, Adrianna. And stopped before they destroy everything we have all been working on for the past twenty-five years. He HAS to be stopped."

"Yes," Adrianna takes a breath, "I know."

"I've already called the…"

"No!" Adrianna said. "I will take care of this."

"Adrianna, the way he's talking about this thing there are going to be more attacks, and soon. He's not trying to make some kind of statement here, Adrianna. He has just declared war. A war against this entire country. We have too…"

"I understand Arthur. I really do. And, as much as I hate to admit it, I think you are right about Klass being involved. I think I always knew this could happen, but I've just hoped… It's the mother thing you know."

"Adrianna.."

"But, I knew this might happen, so I've made arrangements to deal with it, just in case. Let me take those steps now and try to stop this before it goes any further."

Silence.

"Adrianna, you need to understand the situation this puts me in. I was happy to bring Klass onboard when he took on that project your husband gave him. He understood our beliefs. And he understood our goals for the changes we are going to make in the country. And he started out doing some really good work. But as time went on he started talking with some of the other nationalist groups, some of the more radical ones."

"I know."

"I warned him about them. But he went ahead and kept hanging out with them until it was becoming a problem and I had to put some pressure on him to straighten up."

"I know."

"He just laughed at me. He said I didn't understand the true word of God. He went off and joined one of those radical groups and ended up splitting it and starting his own outfit. Adrianna, we've worked all these years getting people into positions so we can make the changes to create a country that follows Biblical law. That's why I ran for this office. But what Klass is doing now will destroy all of that. He's going to fail. You and I both know that. And the result will be a witch hunt against all of us who believe in following scripture. I cannot allow that to happen, Adrianna, I just cannot allow that to happen."

"I understand Arthur. I do."

"Listen Adrianna," the senator said. "Klass needs to be stopped. And if you are not willing to deal with it, then I am going to…"

"That's enough!" Adrianna said. "Arthur, you seem to be forgetting who is responsible for your being in that fancy office you are calling me from."

"I don't…"

"And you seem to forget who it was that put up the money and made the connections so you could create this so-called movement you are worried about."

"No, I…"

"I said that I understand the situation, and I said that I will deal with it. What about that is so difficult to understand?"

Silence.

"No," the Senator said. "I do understand. I'm just concerned."

"Arthur," Adrianna said, "I have as much to lose in this situation as you do, probably more. Klass must be stopped, and I am taking the steps to make that happen. We need to keep our heads about us and work together just like we have up to this point. We can stop what is going on, and I have already begun taking steps to make that happen."

"I understand," the Senator said. "And I appreciate all that you have done; all of it. I guess I'm just worried about how to deal with the pressure I'm going to get when word about this gets out, and…"

"Pressure?" Adrianna said. "Pressure? Arthur, maybe someday I'll tell you what it's like to deal with pressure. But right now, you and I need to keep working together. This is just a temporary problem, Arthur, and it will go away. We need to make sure we are ready to get back to work when it does. Are we good?"

"Yes," the Senator said. "I won't do anything until I hear from you."

"And if you hear any more," Adrianna said. "from Klass or anyone else, you will let me know."

"Yes, of course."

"Fine. I have things to do and will talk with you again later."

Adrianna looked at her phone and pressed the numbers.

Chapter 34

"Hello, mother."

"Klass, are you behind that attack? The one in Illinois?"

"Mother! Not even a nice 'Hello'?"

"Klass, are you..."

"I am a bit busy at the moment mother. We're about to land, and I have dozens of things to do to get ready for tomorrow. But, tell me, how are you?"

"Klass, did you do it?"

"The attack in Springfield? Of course. You know that I did. It's what I have told everyone I was going to do, but no one had enough faith in me to believe I could actually do it. But now you all know."

"Klass, this is not the way to do things."

Silence. Adrianna could not see the smile on Klass' face.

"Klass."

"Mother, this is exactly the way to do things. This is the way God has gone to war against tyrants throughout history. The Amalekites, Assyrians, Babylonians, Egyptians, Hittites, and now the Americans. It is my Father's will, and that is what I must follow."

"Klass, your father never wanted you to..."

"Not him, mother. Not him. Listen, you and dad did the best you knew how to do to raise me. I know that, and I appreciate that. But now, I also know that you did not understand some things, things that were really important. You were distracted by your business things; meetings, money, power, all those things dad tried to teach me and wanted me to do to be just like him. But those are all lies, mother. Those are the things that pull us away from God. Things that end up creating a world that cares more about wealth and power than it does about obeying God's word. We are going to change that world, mother. That is what I am doing. God is using me to create a new nation, a nation truly under God."

"Klass..."

"It took God six days to create the world, mother, and it will take us six days to recreate it. First this country, and then the entire world."

"Klass…"

"I have to go now, mother. One day soon you will understand. And you will be recognized for the role you have played in the fulfilling of God's plan."

"Klass, listen to…"

Click.

Adrianna stared at her phone. She took a deep breath and made the next call.

Chapter 35

"Graham," Emily said.

"Emily, Adrianna VanHollings here. I am calling to ask if you have made a decision about what we talked about last night; about your helping me with the problem with my son?"

"I'm sorry, Mrs. VanHollings. No, I really haven't decided yet. I need more time. So much has happened in the last couple of days, you know? And right now I am on the road, it's not a great time to talk. Can I call you back in a few hours?"

"I understand. But Emily, I'm afraid many things are happening around me as well. The situation with my son has become very serious far more quickly than I anticipated."

"I see."

"Emily, I don't mean to press, but things are happening very fast right now and I do not have very much time. It is important for me to know if you are going to help me, Emily. I really need you to help me. I am under a great deal of pressure to do something to stop things before the Sena..., I mean, before someone..."

"Wait, you started to say Senator again. What Senator."

"Never mind, it's not important. What is important is that I protect my son."

"Mrs. VanHollings, if you want me to help you, you are going to have to start telling me what is going on."

Silence.

Mrs. VanHollings?" Emily said.

"I just need to know if..."

"The Senator, Mrs. VanHollings," Emily said, "or this conversation is over."

"Ok, ok," Adrianna VanHollings said. "When Klass started working for his father, it was with a Senator who has some personal beliefs that he is pushing. Religious beliefs. Beliefs about how the country should be run. His goal is to push those beliefs to try and change things about the country. He wants to do it legally, through proper channels, that's why he became a Senator. Klass began to share those beliefs, but unfortunately, he got involved with some of the more radical groups, and he and the Senator parted ways. Now, the Senator is afraid that Klass may do something that will threaten what the Senator is trying to do, so..."

"Wait," Emily said. "What does the Senator think Klass will do? Is this connected to what happened in Kansas, and what just happened in Illinois?"

"All that I know is that if I don't stop Klass, the Senator is going to take steps to stop him. There are many other powerful people with the Senator, and I am afraid of what they will do."

"Wait a second," Emily said as she slowed and pulled her car to the side of the road. "What is the Senator's name?"

"Well, I don't believe I..."

"Let me guess, is it Arthur Murena?"

"How ever did you know that?"

"Let's just say the Senator and I have met before, and that I am familiar with his, uh, beliefs. We go way back."

"So, will you help me?" Adrianna said.

"I have one more question," Emily said. "Yes or no; is Klass involved in what happened in Kansas and Illinois?"

Silence.

"Last chance," Emily said.

"Yes," Adrianna VanHollings said. "I am afraid he is. Now, will you work with us and help me save my son?"

"Mrs. VanHollings, I have every intention of stopping Klass, but I will do it on my own. I am through joining things."

"Thank you, Emily," Adrianna said. "But if there is anything..."

Click.

Chapter 36

      The area of the Capital complex glowed from the mobile light towers, some brought from Decatur, Jacksonville, even as far away as St. Louis, along with the white, red, blue, and yellow flashing lights from the emergency response vehicles parked along the streets. The only light coming from inside any of the buildings was the occasional flash in a window from one of the search parties checking every room of every building for someone needing help. Others searched basements, while still others walked the miles of tunnels below the complex.

      Several powerful portable LED units glared from inside the yellow tape that marked the secure boundary around the delivery van parked between the Illinois Supreme Court and the Illinois State Bar Association buildings. They lit-up the jackets identifying teams from the Illinois Emergency Management Agency, Homeland Security, the FBI, and more. Members of the Illinois National Guard, in full response gear, lined the yellow tape. Units of the Springfield Police Department and the Illinois State Police were located at every corner, while others patrolled the entire area fully prepared to deal with anyone attempting to take advantage of the situation.

      Some cell phones and radios worked, while others did not; it all depended on how far away the tower was. Larry Renshaw had been dealing with that for the past fourteen hours, but now sat on the floor of the communications station, leaning against the basement wall and staring at the racks of dead equipment. Things were still crashing around him, but those pieces that had survived the initial hit could be restarted. Those units that went down at the beginning could not. Whatever had hit those pieces had not just shut them down, it had cooked them. When those first units when down, the system tried to adjust by rerouting things, causing overloads on other units, leading to more outages, and more overloads. When this cascade began to take down other systems across Central Illinois, the decision was made to take the entire building off-line. It would stop most all wireless or radio communication in the area, but the cascade had to be stopped. While Larry and the other techs tried to fix things downstairs, the suits upstairs studied the maps to try and figure out how to get service back by rerouting the entire system to avoid the parts connected to the capitol complex. Until they did, the area was without cell phones, without medical telemetry, without Internet, and without 911.

Chuck Donahue had locked the post office doors after making sure everything was a secure as he could make it. He spent the day helping open unresponsive automatic doors, helping direct people to the evacuation area, and pushing vehicles out of the way to make room for emergency vehicles. Chuck was now holding a flashlight, leading one of the groups looking for people caught in the miles of now unlit tunnels under the complex.

Kinsey Elliott had walked seven blocks to find a working phone and call the Senator back. She spent the past fourteen hours finding a location where she could work.

Walter Beaton sat in his truck in the parking lot behind the Illinois State Library, just across the street from the Supreme Court Building. An amateur radio operator, Walter had gone home to his gear and contact other "hams" who were now located in key areas around the complex helping provide communications for the responders.

Denosha Morgan drove her third ambulance of the day down East Capitol with one of the amateur radio operators riding shotgun to take the calls. She had performed CPR four more times since the unsuccessful one this morning.

Lanna Gilbert sat at her kitchen table with her husband. She was still dizzy from the panic attack she suffered during her nine hours in the dark elevator.

Kyle Bagshaw had moved from the barstool to a table near the window where he stared at the train still sitting on the tracks. He thought about maybe someday just climbing onto one of those cars as it passed by and see where it might take him. Then he got another beer.

Klass VanHollings was on his plane parked outside a hanger on the North side of the airport runways in St. Louis. His jet had all of the luxuries of the best hotels, without the hassles. He celebrated the day with steak dinner brought from his favorite downtown chef, personal time in Bible study and prayer, and was now enjoying the company of a very attractive young woman.

There was very little traffic on Missouri State Route 37 as the two unmarked semis drove around Cassville on their way to I-44.

Chapter 37

"Hi, Em. How you doing?"

"How did you know it was me?" Emily said. "I'm on a hotel phone."

"Seriously?" Liz said. "It's not tough. My computer is tied into both the cell and landline systems, so when I get a call from a landline my computer locates it and then searches for cell phones within a range of that location. Yours was the closest. No biggie."

"Geez, when did the agency get that? I hadn't heard of it."

"Nope, this is mine. I'm not sure I trust the agency with it yet. What can I do for you, and what are you doing in Illinois? Because of that attack? You back with the agency? Damn, I hated to hear what they did to you. It sucks."

"Thanks," Emily said. "Yes, I'm in Illinois, but no, I'm not with the agency. I'm here because...well, I'm just here, let's leave it at that. Liz, there's something I'd like you to do for me if you can. Are you still okay with helping, even though I'm not inside anymore?"

"Who do you want nuked? Just name 'em. I'll teach 'em to screw with my friend."

"No, nothing like that. But thanks. I want some information about someone. Just information for now. A senator."

"A senator? Awesome! Which one?"

"Arthur Murena," Emily said.

"Murena?" Liz said. "Got it. What do you want to know about him?"

"First, I want his schedule so I know where I can find him if I need to. Then, anything else you can find; what he's been working on, who he's hanging out with..."

"Wow, this guy has got some authentic weirdness going on," Liz said.

"What do you mean? How do you know that?"

"I just ran a quick thing on him on my computer. He's got some interesting friends on the dark web, is that what you're looking for?"

"What kind of friends?"

"Funky kinds. Off-the-wall religious kinds, white supremacist kinds. He's into some really heavy stuff. This guy's a senator?"

"Yeah," Emily said. "But, I already know about his, uh, beliefs. I want to know who he's making nice with, who he's hanging with, who is providing him with any unofficial contributions. But the schedule first, okay? Can you get that to me in the morning?"

"Give me ten minutes and I'll…"

"No, morning is fine. I need to get some sleep. And Liz, not the public schedule. I need his real one."

"No prob," Liz said. "Hey, are you okay? I mean, with your dad and all. I was sorry to hear about that."

"Yeah, I'll be fine, thanks. Oh, one more thing?"

"Name it."

"Is there a way to check to see if anyone has been tracking my phone again, I mean like you said they were doing before?"

"Nah," Liz said. "You don't need to worry about that. I fixed it so nobody can track that phone, or monitor it, or anything like that. Nobody can tag that phone anymore."

"Then how did you…"

"Nobody but me, of course. Because…"

"Because you are the Lizard!"

"Absafreakinlootly!"

"Thanks, Liz."

"Anytime. Get some sleep."

Emily stretched out on the bed and turned on the television. She flipped through channels until she came to the public channel and the two people doing the usual fund-raising thing. She was about to turn the thing off when one of them mentioned they were ready to go back to the 1985 Jimmy Buffett concert at Red Rocks. Emily put the remote down, eased her head back on her pillow, and smiled. She was growing drowsy as Jimmy started singing 'If The Phone Doesn't Ring It's Me'. She saw her phone floating over her head, blowing back and forth in the wind like a kite. She watched Liz walk across the beach and cut the string, letting the phone fly away. In the distance down the beach, she saw the senator standing with a crowd of people wearing dark masks, talking with Klass and his mother and all looking in her direction. And in the two chairs next to Emily sat her mom and dad, surrounded by of all the dogs.

Chapter 38

""Let's get the vans unloaded and start up the road. We're only about twenty miles out, but there will be traffic this time of the morning."

The men opened the doors of the two semi-trailers and drove the two smaller delivery vans and two cars out into the warehouse.

"Both devices are ready?" Walter said.

"I've checked them both," Ralph said. "The timers are set. They just need to be armed when we get to the locations."

"And everyone knows where to meet-up after?"

"Ditch the cars in the airport long-term parking and take the shuttle around to the hangars, yeah."

"Good. And drivers," Walter said, "remember to stay at least a half-mile apart from each other on the road. Our group will leave first, and you guys start out in an hour. Since we have further to go, that should put both of us in place at about the same time. Just everybody be careful, okay?"

"Relax, Walt," Chuck said. "We're ready for this. Let's have a prayer before we go."

Minutes later, the first of the two vans pulled out of the building in the industrial complex East of Peerless Park and pulled onto Eastbound Interstate 44 towards St. Louis. The getaway car followed behind the van. The morning traffic was heavy, so they found their places in the line and did their best to blend in.

Chapter 39

"Hey, you can't park there!" Emily heard the shout as she got out of her car.

Emily started to reach for her badge but remembered it was still in New Orleans. The man walked toward her with a determined look on his face, until he glanced in the back window of the car and saw Emily's jacket on the back seat.

"Oh, I didn't realize you were FBI," the man said. "You need to park here very long?"

"Uh, no," Emily said. "I'm just checking on some things."

"Okay, go ahead and leave it there, then," the man said. "I'm sorry for yelling at you, but with all the people showing up around here I just got tired of them taking up the spaces. You didn't have a sticker, but yeah, it's okay to leave it there for a while."

"Thanks," Emily said. "I'll move it as soon as I can."

Emily walked up Fourth Street and turned left on Jackson. She pulled the little notebook out of her pocket. Reporters could go most anywhere without anyone paying any attention to them, and that was the amount of attention she wanted to attract this morning. She walked along the yellow tape and the activities inside it and crossed Second Street to the Capital Building. She stood on the lawn trying to understand the scope of what had happened. She saw a man sitting under a nearby tree, with a hardhat and large tool belt on the ground beside him.

"What a mess, huh?" Emily said.

"You got that right," the man said.

"You been working on things here?" she said, nodding towards his hat and belt.

"Yeah, I guess you could say that. Damndest thing I've ever seen, I'll tell you that."

"That bad?"

"Bad?" he said. "Here in the capitol, we've been swapping out breakers, replacing fuses, switches, transformers, things like that. We've replaced anything we've found that needed replacing, and that's pretty much everything in the building."

"Really?"

"I think we've got things ready for whenever they can get power on again, we'll see."

"That's good."

"Yeah, but we're the lucky ones. Hell of a lot luckier than what those guys are dealing with across the street."

"Across the street?" Emily said.

"Yeah, the buildings right next to the truck thing. They've replaced everything like we have but it hasn't done any good. All of the wiring in those buildings looks just fine. No breaks, nothing. There's just one problem."

"What's that."

"They won't carry no power."

"What, the wiring?"

"Yeah. It's all still there, but it just won't carry. It won't conduct. It's like they're going to have to replace every foot of wire in every building over there. You got any idea what that's gonna amount to?"

"I can't imagine."

"Well, I can," the man said. "And it ain't pretty."

"What would cause something like that?" Emily said.

"Something fried it, that's for sure. Just kinda melted it or something. I've seen a direct lightning hit do things like that, but never seen anything this big."

Emily looked at the buildings.

"Tell you what I'd like," the man said. "I'd like to find the people who did this and get them in a room for about five minutes, that's what I'd like."

Emily looked across the street still trying to imagine what the man was describing.

"Well," he said, "I'd better get back to it. Nice talkin' with ya'."

"You too," Emily said. "You be careful."

"The only way," he said as he walked up the steps and entered the dark capitol building.

Emily walked across the lawn to Monroe Street looking for anything that might spark some insight into what happened here yesterday morning. She was approaching the corner when she first saw him.

He was wearing a cowboy hat and standing under a tree watching the yellow tape. First, it occurred to Emily that his was the only cowboy hat she had seen in the entire city so far. And second, he wasn't watching the yellow tape, he was staring at it, studying it, collecting every piece of data he could collect about what was taking place behind the yellow tape.

She watched as he crossed Second Street and walked toward railroad tracks. What struck her was that he wasn't just walking, he moved like someone who knew how to not be noticed, someone who knew how to blend in and get into places he wasn't supposed to be. He followed the tracks until he was on the opposite side of the area with the yellow tape. From there, he had a clear view of the activities, and the van. Emily found a spot under some trees where she could get a good look at the yellow tape, and still keep an eye on the cowboy hat.

From the distance, Emily guessed he was Caucasian, probably in his thirties, about six-foot to six-two, maybe 180 pounds give or take, and clearly had some military training. Or worse.

"They always come back to see what they have done," Emily said to herself. "The idiots always come back."

Chapter 40

"Morning Ronnie," Grandpa said. "Looks like I beat you this morning."

"Yeah," Ronnie said as he sat down. "Looks like it."

"What's the matter? Something bothering you? The kids okay?"

Ronnie drank from his coffee.

"Oh, yeah, the kids are fine. They're fine."

"Then what is it? Are you still thinking about what happened to your contact?"

"No, it's not that. I've just been thinking about some things. About the group; our group. Trying to figure some things out. But we have other things we probably ought to talk about this morning. Like Illinois."

"Yes, but first tell me what's bothering you. I need you focused and not distracted by something else. What are you trying to figure out?"

"Well, for one thing, this woman, Emily Graham. How did she get so involved in the things we are doing? I mean, you said we don't like to use the same people more than once, but she's been involved in a lot more than that. Why? And how did she get involved in the first place?"

Grandpa drank from his coffee as he looked at Ronnie.

"I've been thinking it was time we talked about that. Not just about Graham, but how the process works. I've been waiting until I felt it was time to do that. I guess it's time."

"What process?"

"Ronnie, what I'm going to tell you may be difficult to understand at first. That's why I've waited. I thought the more familiar you were with why we do what we do, the easier it would be to understand. So, just listen to all of what I have to say before you make up your mind about any of it, okay?"

"Sure, but I..."

"Ronnie, to do the things our group does, we have to always be looking for people who may be able to help us. People who can do the things we need our influencers to do."

"Influencers?"

"That's what we call them. Since we can't risk trying to do things directly ourselves, these are the people we use to influence what happens; influence decisions that are made, actions that are taken. They are the people our contacts communicate with. Contacts like your Steve. But unlike contacts, when we identify a really useful influencer, we may use them more than once when the situation calls for it."

"So Graham is one of the influencers," Ronnie said. "Okay, how did that happen? Why her?"

"Like I said, we are always looking for people who might have the skills needed. In Graham's case, we first noticed her while she was still in school. She was..."

"School?" Ronnie said. "What, college?"

"No," Grandpa said. "For her, it was Junior High, I believe. We monitor the various tests that are given and watch for those individuals who show the potential for developing the skills needed to be an influencer. Skills like..."

"Wait," Ronnie said. "Wait. You mean those tests that my kids are taking in school? The tests I took in school? That's not what you're talking about monitoring? Those tests?"

"That's exactly what I am talking about, Ronnie. We monitor..."

"But, but, wait! I thought those were confidential, at least that's what they all say. And they give those to measure academic things, not..."

"Ronnie, like I said earlier, listen to everything I have to tell you before you make up your mind about any of it. Yes, the tests are for academics, but they tell us a lot more. And as for confidentiality, yes, that too. Except for us."

"The group is monitoring my kids?" Ronnie said.

"We are always watching for individuals who may be worth further monitoring. For influencers, we are looking for those who may have good academic abilities, but other things may be more important. Like skills in perception and problem-solving. The ability to find connections between things that may not appear to be connected. The ability to notice things others might miss, and understand things about situations and people that others might not understand."

Ronnie stared at his coffee.

"Ronnie," Grandpa said. "Have you ever looked at the tests your kids are taking and wondered about them? I mean, have you ever wondered why some of the questions were so vague, and sometimes just outright confusing?"

"Yeah, I just assumed the companies that designed them were lousy educators."

"Well, sometimes that may be true. But no, the reason is that we want to see how the test takers will deal with things that don't make sense. To see how well they can make sense of them, and how they go about doing that. Take Emily Graham for example. Her tests in Junior High showed she had the skills I mentioned, along with a level of stubbornness that made her spend the time to try and make sense of the confusing questions. That stubbornness is one of the things we look for the most."

"Why?"

"It means that if that person ever ends up in a situation where someone is trying to sway their opinion, force them to do something they don't want to do, or trying to stop them from doing what they need to do, they are less likely give in. It means..."

"Okay," Ronnie said. "Okay. I understand. But I'm just not sure I like the idea that kids are being monitored like this. Watched. And without their parents knowing about it. It's just not right."

"But it is necessary if we are going to do the job we need to do. But let me finish."

"Yeah."

"When we find someone like Graham, someone with the potential skills, we keep monitoring them as they continue their education. And, when we think it is helpful, we provide influences that will help them further develop those skills, and give them opportunities to expand their..."

"Wait. Influences? For kids?"

"When we believe it is appropriate. And that is what is important, Ronnie. We aren't treating them like puppets on strings. We simply do things that give them opportunities they can choose from, opportunities that would not come along if we did not open the doors. We never take control of someone's life. We offer choices."

"Like what?"

"Like a college, for one thing, one they would never have considered. Or maybe entice them to try a new subject area, or interact with a new group of people, or even read a new book. All kinds of things that will help them further develop their abilities to become..."

"To become what we want them to become," Ronnie said.

Grandpa smiled and drank.

"Yes, Ronnie. I know it looks that bad. But again, we never force them to do anything. We never in any way take away their freedom of choice."

"We just control their choices," Ronnie said.

"No!" Grandpa said. "We do not control. We offer choices."

Ronnie stood, walked to the counter for another coffee, sat back down and stared out the window.

"What are you thinking?" Grandpa said.

"I don't know, Grandpa. I mean, about all of this now. I just don't know."

"Ronnie, I know you may not believe me, but I felt exactly the same way when I was told about this. So, I do understand."

"So," Ronnie looked his Grandfather in the eyes, "was I monitored too? Have you been watching and, influencing me too?"

"Yes," Grandpa said. "We have..."

"So then tell me this, Grandpa. How much of all that stuff that happened, the things we did together, the stories you told me, the places we went together, how many of those were real, and how many of those were just you and the group giving me opportunities? How many?"

The old man looked much older. His eyes became glassy.

"Ronnie, everything we did, that I did, all of it, was because of how much I loved you, and how much I wanted you to know that you were loved too. All of it. Yes, I saw the strengths you had. And, yes, I watched and hoped that someday you might be able to join me in this role. But it was all real. Whatever else may have come from it, all of those things were just me and you. I do hope you can believe that."

"I want to, Grandpa. I do. But right now I think I need to go. I need--I just need to go. Unless there is something the group needs that is more important?"

Ronnie stood.

"No," Grandpa said. "I will handle things. I will see you in the morning?"

His grandson had already turned toward the door.

Chapter 41

Daryl spent the night in the I-55 rest area thirty miles South of Springfield. He could have gone the rest of the way, but he was not in the mood to deal with people. He found an open spot to park, set his duffel up as a pillow, and slept in his truck. He just needed some time to think. He had thought middle-of-nowhere Kansas was the solution he was looking for. It was probably foolish to pack-up and leave like he did, but there was something about what had happened in Springfield that he just had to sort through. Whatever authority he might have relied on in Kansas would not be recognized here, even if he hadn't given it up with that text message. He had no clear agenda. He just had to go there.

Daryl parked his truck several blocks away from downtown on a street that gave him a clear and secure path back out of the area. That probably wasn't needed in this situation, but old habits sometimes served a purpose. He looked at the numbers of official-looking vehicles parked in along the streets as he neared the capitol complex. He was familiar with most of those outfits and had spent time working or arguing with most of them at one time or another. He wondered for a moment if he might run into someone who would recognize him and if that would be a good or bad thing.

Daryl noticed when the traffic lights and other electrical devices stopped working. He estimated the line was something like eight hundred yards from the capitol building itself. As he walked across the Capital lawn and saw the yellow tape, he decided that the actual impact of the device must have reached right at one thousand yards. He shook his head.

"A big one," Daryl said to himself.

He was not wearing a uniform and did not have tools, but Daryl had found that if you show-up someplace wearing a cowboy hat, people tend to think you belong, like maybe your one of those Texas Rangers or something like that. He walked up the steps to the capitol building and nodded at the security guard. The guard opened the door.

"Here you go, sir," the guard said.

"Thanks," Daryl said as he tapped the brim of his hat.

He walked a few of the darkened hallways and talked with two or three of the engineers and electricians gathered here and there. It was either the hat, or just the way he acted like he belonged, but they all talked with him and explained what they were discovering about the attack. Daryl understood what they were describing far better than any of them imagined. As he walked out of the building's East door, he saw her.

She was chatting-up an electrician taking a break. She was carrying a reporter's notebook, but never took a note. Not one.

"Busted!", Daryl said to himself.

Daryl stepped back into the Capitol Building and then out the Northern door so he could keep an eye on her without her seeing him. He had just come out of the door when she stopped talking to the electrician and started walking in his direction. He ducked behind the stairway, and after she passed he walked toward the corner and found a place he could track her from behind a tree.

"So, doing a bit of snoopin', are we darlin'," Daryl said to himself.

That's when he got distracted.

Daryl had glanced across Second Street and noticed the yellow tape. He searched for something meaningful but all he saw was the tape and the uniforms guarding it. More damn uniforms. He walked South along the sidewalk to get a better look, but the trees and buildings hid everything. Finally, Daryl walked back to the corner and made his way around the block until he was standing on the opposite side of the buildings, with a clear view of the tape, and the van. The van was partially covered with a tent, but Daryl saw enough to understand why it was there.

"A thousand yards," he said to himself.

He turned and looked around to estimate just how far that would actually reach from the truck when he saw her looking in his direction.

"Shit," he said to himself.

Chapter 42

"There's our turn," Walter said.

"Yeah," Stu said. "I'm glad traffic eased-up after we got past the arch back there. I was afraid we were gonna get behind schedule."

The van took the Broadway exit and slowed for the stoplight.

"Hang a left," Walter said, "then right at the next light."

They turned on to Carrie Avenue and drove past the restaurants at the truck stop.

"Wow," Walter said. "Look at the trucks. Food must be good, cause the gas isn't cheap."

Yeah," Stu said, "and now I'm hungry."

"We'll eat on the plane," Walter said. "We're almost there. Turn right after this train track."

"Yep," Stu said. "Sure doesn't look like much of a street though."

Third Street ran between the tracks and a large parking area filled with semi-trailers, then curved to go through the buildings and tracks of the railroad's maintenance yard.

"Hey," Stu said, "there's one of those roundhouses over there. Don't see many of those around anymore."

"Yeah," Walter said. "Okay, I think we've got something here. Stay cool."

As they drove between the buildings and the rows of tracks, Walter saw the man standing in the road about thirty feet in front of them. Stu stopped and opened the window as the man walked up.

"You fella's lost?" the man said.

"Yeah, looking for the Division Office," Walter said. "I think we turned too early."

"That's what I figured," the man said. "Just go left between that second row of trailers there. You'll see the office in front of you."

"Yeah, thanks!" Walter said as he looked at Stu and nodded toward the trailers.

Walter watched the man in the mirror as they drove.

"He's gone," Walter said. "Turn here, down this row."

They drove through the yard until they came to the spot halfway between the Division Office and the yard's control tower.

"Here," Walter said. "Right along the fence there. You go raise the hood while I arm the device."

Three minutes later Walter and Stu climbed into the backseat of the car waiting for them on Hall Street.

Chapter 43

"Yeah, a big white one," Emily said. "Looks like he's trying to be a Texas Ranger or something."

"And he's just looking around?"

"Yeah, so far."

"Well, just keep an eye on him. I'll see if I can find out anything that might help identify him. What else?"

"Had another conversation with VanHollings, the wife. She confirmed that her son, Klass, is involved in the attacks. As concerned as she is about stopping him, I don't think she's involved too."

"Okay, what have you found out about the attacks themselves?"

"All I can tell you is that, whatever these things are doing, they are not just knocking stuff out for a while. An electrician told me they were going to have to completely rewire the buildings closest to the truck. The wiring just doesn't work anymore. I haven't gotten a good look at the van yet, the one with the thing in it. That's going to be a bit tough. I'd sure like too, though."

"Sounds like some kind of EMP alright," Chambers said. "Just like Lance said. Be careful and don't do anything stupid, you know?"

"Yeah," Emily said. "You got anything else for me?"

"I heard from your buddy, Dasilva, this morning."

"Super Agent called you? And what did he have to say?"

"He wanted me to tell you how sorry he was about what happened, and that he wasn't able to help you."

"Yeah," Emily said. "Tell him I'll keep him on my Christmas card list."

"And he told me to tell you to watch your back. He said some really strange things are going on in the offices above his. He said there were some kind of pressures coming from some Senator or something, but wouldn't tell me more than that. And, he said he doesn't think what happened to you is over yet. So keep an eye open."

"Yeah," Emily said. "I will. My good one."

"Anything I need to know about all that?" Chambers said. "The part about the senator, maybe?"

"Not now. I'll let you know."

"Oh," Chambers said. "Dasilva also wanted me to tell you that he put the box inside your door at your house. And he said he put a little something extra in it for you. If that makes any sense at all."

"Yeah, the box has the stuff from my office. Super Agent was kind enough to pack it up for me."

"Oh, okay."

"Gotta go," Emily said. "I'll let you know when I have more."

"Okay," Chambers said. "And, oh, Graham. One more thing?"

"Yeah?"

"Don't go trying to be a hero, okay?"

"Nah, cult legend will be good enough for me."

"Graham..."

Chapter 44

"Good morning, Senator. How nice of you to take my call."

"This is not the way to do things, Klass. This is not how to make the changes you…"

"I know, Senator, I know. You told me that three years ago when you threw me out of your office,"

"Klass, I was only trying to…"

"Senator! I did not call to argue with you this morning. There is no reason for us to be at odds any longer. Not now. I am calling to suggest that you keep an eye on the news this morning. You are going to see things that will help you understand what I am going to tell you when I call you again this afternoon. It will help you understand what you are going to need to do."

"What are you…"

"Until later, Senator," Klass said.

Klass put his phone on the table and ate the last piece of toast from his plate. He got up from his chair, knelt on the floor near the sofa, and prayed. Tears ran down his cheeks as he gave thanks for the gifts he had been given, and the opportunity to demonstrate those gifts again this morning. He prayed for the safety of his followers, and for all of those pure and loyal believers in the one, true, word of God. He stood, walked to the bedroom at the rear of the plane, and put on his sweater and jacket.

"You can go now," Klass said to the young woman still lying on his bed as he left the room and stepped from the plane.

Klass joined the small group standing outside the hangar. They joined hands and bowed their heads for a brief prayer before Klass stepped away from the group, turned to face the direction of the rail yard, and raise his arms high in the air.

Chapter 45

"Just who the hell are you, anyway," Emily said to herself as she watched the cowboy standing with the crowd of gawkers across the tracks from the yellow tape.

She shook her head and mumbled, "That stupid hat makes you stick out like balls on a bullfrog."

Emily smiled as she heard one of her dad's favorite phrases come out of her mouth. It was one of the tamer ones. She thought about how he liked to embarrass her mother by throwing out one of his comments at the most inappropriate time. And she remembered the arguments that followed when they got back home. There were a lot of arguments, and most of them were caused by one of them doing something to piss the other off. When she was younger and still trapped there, living with them, she wondered why they were that stupid to constantly go out of their way to make everyone in the house so miserable. Now, she wonders if some couples just enjoy fighting, and she was the only one in the house in misery? But all that was part of what made her, her. She remembered the night she sat in her room listening to the yelling and made the decision that, when she finally escaped, her world was not going to include that kind of nonsense.

Emily was so far back in that dark bedroom, she didn't hear him walk up behind her.

"Emily," he said.

She whirled around in a perfect, front-kick posture.

"Steve!" she said as she lowered her arms. "You scared the hell out of me. What are you doing here?"

"You need to go, Emily," Steve said. "Now. You are being followed, and from what we've been able to find out about them, you are not safe here. You need to..."

"Who is..."

"Listen, Emily. These people are dangerous. There is help coming, but we don't have time. You need to go!"

Emily glanced at the yellow tape, and the van, and the cowboy hat.

"Emily! Listen to me. You need to go."

"Where?" Emily said. "Just where do you expect me to go?"

"Someplace where it would be difficult for anyone to get near you without your seeing them. Someplace out, someplace like the cabin."

Emily stiffened.

"How do you know about that?"

"Just go," Steve said. "You need to go there. You need to get out of here, and NOW!"

She looked and saw the cowboy hat was still there. She turned back and she was alone.

Emily let out a deep breath and started walking to her car.

Chapter 46

The lights in the railroad offices did not flicker, they just went out. Along with the computers, the air conditioning, the phones, and the microwave oven heating Carol's coffee.

"Hey, what's going on?" Carol said.

Jim Dinley was in the trench beneath the locomotive, completing his inspection and holding the utility light as Paul reconnected hoses. Then it was dark.

Two mechanics were using a hydraulic hoist to position a new fan unit into the engine compartment of another locomotive. The compressor for the hoist stopped running at the same instant the light disappeared.

Wayne had been watching things from his window in the tower at the North end of the yard. His crews were busy sorting cars, breaking the trains that had just come in, and staging a half-dozen others to send out. It was a routine morning, but as Yardmaster, Wayne had to pay close attention to all of it to keep things on schedule and avoid the call from the front office when he didn't.

When his panel first went dark, Wayne assumed it was just a blip. That sometimes happened, since many pieces of the equipment had some age on them. But Wayne noticed the wall lights for the track sensors and switch controllers were off as well. When he looked out the window he saw the track lights were dark, and his locomotives were stopped, their confused crews looking up in his direction. As much as he hated the idea, he picked up the phone to call the office. The phone was dead. He picked up his cell phone. Same thing. Wayne's mind began to race as he ran through the list of all of the things in his yard that, without power, were no longer working.

Chapter 47

"Okay, darlin', want to play a little cat and mouse with me, huh?"

Daryl stood next to the building where he could see the van, and watch the snoop through the reflection on the building's front window. He thought about the time he had used that in Saudi. Or was it Kiev?

She had followed him around the building and had been watching from the trees next to the sidewalk. She was good. If he hadn't noticed the unused notebook, he would never have given her a second thought. Not about the attack anyway, and this wasn't the time to think about other options. She clearly had some training. Maybe military, but whose? And why was she tailing him? What if that electrician under the tree wasn't an electrician at all? What if..."

"Get a grip Daryl!" he said.

People turned to look. He smiled and shrugged.

Then he saw the man approach her, and her reaction. Daryl watched their conversation as he began slowly moving in their direction. He had no idea why, but there was something about this that ate at him. If she was following him, and she was not alone, what the hell was she up too? And who is the guy with her? And why does it look like they are arguing?

He was still moving in their direction when he saw her glance in his direction, turn, and walk away. Fast. The guy she had been talking with was gone.

Daryl stopped.

As it had done hundreds of times before, his mind ran through the options, sorting them by probability and level of risk, looking for the most viable next step.

Maybe she is just a reporter, just not a good one. Maybe she is just looking for a story and thought I might be one.

Maybe she is a cop who thinks I'm one of the bad guys.

Maybe she is one of the attackers, back to evaluate the damage done so they learn from it.

Maybe she is just a snoop, getting her kicks.

Maybe she is...

"Well, shit!" Daryl said as he took one more quick look at the yellow tape and followed the snoop down the sidewalk.

Chapter 48

The drive from the warehouse near Peerless had been quiet until they turned onto Chouteau Avenue from Jefferson.

"So far, so good," Chuck said as he made the turn.

"Just like we planned it, huh?" Ralph said.

It was quiet again as they made the left turn onto Twenty-First. They drove past the two entrances into the building's parking area, and followed the signs all the way around to the company's shipping and receiving area.

"Amazing!" Chuck said.

"What?" Ralph said. "What's amazing?"

"That it's this easy to get in here like this. I mean, you would think an outfit like this would make it a little harder to just drive in like this. I mean, what are they thinking?"

"Like Klass says," Ralph said, "people today are thinking about things that don't really matter, and completely ignoring the things that do. That's what we're going to change."

"Yeah, but man, I mean, look how easy this is!"

"Park over there," Ralph said. "One of those spaces between the building and the big A-C units there. I'll get the thing armed."

Two minutes later, the got in the car waiting for them in the parking lot. Chuck turned to look at the corporate building.

"Amazing!" he said.

Chapter 49

"Hey, Liz, you have any luck with that schedule for me?"

"You okay?" Liz said. "You sound out of breath? Not enjoying some…"

"No," Emily said. "Nothing like that. Just walking to my car. Apparently, I have company up here, and I've been told I need to go somewhere to hide. Can you believe that?"

"Damn!" Liz said. "You need some help? Anything I can do?"

"Not now, thanks. Just that schedule if…"

"Already on your phone," Liz said. "Sent it last night."

"Oh, sorry, I didn't see it. I've been focused on other things."

"You sure you don't…"

"Gotta go. Don't worry, I'm fine. Thanks, Liz."

Emily put the phone in her pocket and got in the car. She waved at the man guarding the drive as she pulled away. She made a stop to fill up the tank and then headed West out of Springfield toward the cabin, and her past. Forty minutes later, she turned onto the gravel road, following the turns she somehow remembered. Then she was there. She got out, stood at the side of her car, and looked around.

It was nighttime the last time she had been here, and she hadn't realized how much things had changed. Where there used to be trees and water, now there were cornfields. And everything seemed smaller than it used to be. She reached in her pocket for the key her dad had given her the day he bought the cabin. They each got their own key; dad, mom, and Emily. He bought it to be their escape. It was to be a place they could do and be whatever they wanted to do and be. No boat crew to deal with, no HR department, just them. It was to be their spot. But mom never really liked the place. When she first saw it she made a list of all the things she was going to fix-up. That led to another argument. Dad said this was supposed to be their escape, not their resort condo. And if they did the things on her list to gussy it all up, hell, people would want to come out and spend time there too, and that was not at all what he had in mind. So, mom came to the cabin three times. That first day they bought it, the day they had the party for Emily's high school graduation, and the day she and dad took that one last drive around the countryside before she died.

After that, dad came out here when he was off the boat, and when he retired he sold the house and moved into the cabin for good. He was there until the night she came to take him to the South where he would be close enough for her to keep an eye on him. She walked to the spot where he stood that night and took his last look. Fortunately for him, in his mind, she was there to take him to meet one of his boats. Emily was the only one who had to deal with the reality of what was happening.

Inside, everything was the same as they left it that night. She put her bag in the big living room, looked in the freezer for something to eat, and started cleaning things up enough to cook.

After eating, she walked around the cabin and went in to his room. In the rush, things that did not have to make the trip South were tossed on the bed or the dresser, or the floor. She straightened things up a bit to keep her mind busy and avoid thinking about why she was here. Running and hiding felt too much like crying.

She opened the dresser drawers and dug through things. She wasn't sure what she might be looking for. She opened the bottom drawer and saw the box. It had a pink ribbon tied around it. It looked completely out of place surrounded by the shotgun shells, a leaking bottle of gun oil, an old hunting magazine, a torn sweatshirt, and a 357 Magnum, loaded. She took the box out of the drawer, untied the ribbon, and opened it. It was stuffed with old envelopes, cards, newspaper clippings, photos, and a few bits and pieces she couldn't identify. She pulled out one of the envelopes and held it up. Emily had to sit down.

It was the letter she had written to him when she was in college, that day she had decided to tell him how much she had been hurt by all of their arguing. She had written it to show him that she was now all grown-up and strong enough to stand on her own. But, as soon as she mailed it, she realized it was just cruel. It was a childish attempt to get even, nothing more. Over all the years, he had never mentioned that letter. Never. She had hoped it had somehow gotten lost in the mail and that he had never read it. Had never read the letter she now held in her hands, the envelop opened, and the paper weak from being unfolded and folded again, and again.

Tears.

Emily hated to cry. Even if there were good reasons for tears, it always felt like giving up, like failure, like something someone would do who was not able to handle things. The only time she had seen her mother cry was during the arguments. She couldn't remember ever seeing him cry.

She carried the box into the living room table. There were report cards, graduation announcements, ribbons from things she didn't remember, letters from summer camps, newspaper articles about the day she entered the academy, headlines of her various activities in the agency, and at least one photo of her from every year until she left for college. And her mother's wedding ring, with a strand of her mother's hair knotted around it.

Chapter 50

"Yes, she is here," the voice on the phone said, "in Springfield."

"You saw her yourself?" Klass said.

"Yes, and she is not alone."

"What do you mean? Who is with her?"

"I'm not sure yet. At least two. One of them is someone we saw her with at that nursing home in New Orleans. And I don't know if she's actually with the other guy, but they seem to be moving around together."

"She just doesn't give up, does she?" Klass smiled. "Where is she right now?"

"We don't know. She got in a car and left before we could get back to ours. It looked like one of the others was following her."

"I don't understand the problem. She's bound to have her phone with her, aren't you tracking that?"

"We've tried. Several times. We just can't get it. But we'll..."

Klass smiled.

"No," Klass said. "Never mind. Don't waste your time. Clearly, she is too smart for that. But keep looking, she is going to show up someplace again. She isn't the type to run and hide for long."

Klass handed the phone to one of the men standing around him.

"She is something else," Klass said. "I wish there was a way-- well, I'll pray about it later. Let's do this."

The group joined hands for a prayer, and then watched as Klass turned to face downtown St. Louis, and raised his arms.

Chapter 51

Ambulances came and went as the emergency responders dealt with the injuries in the maintenance building caused by equipment that failed or malfunctioned when the electrical power that controlled them stopped.

Nothing moved in the rail yard. The Yardmaster's crew chiefs met at the tower to come up with a way to get the critical work done to try and reduce the losses that a complete stoppage would create. The Yardmaster himself walked to the division office and met with the execs to go over the emergency response plan and make sure everything they had trained for was being carried out.

The IT team went through their network systems to determine how much damage had been done, and what parts of that damage could be repaired, and how quickly. Two members of the IT team argued about how the backup drives stored in the fully secure, electrical-interference-proof, storage unit had been erased.

Across the Midwest, rail traffic controllers struggled to re-route and re-schedule trains to keep as much cargo moving as possible. Railyards throughout the Midwest began to back-up with trains and trucks waiting to pick-up or deliver their loads.

Five miles to the South, a corporate trainer displayed slide number thirty-seven of her PowerPoint presentation explaining the changes taking place because of the new HR policies regarding workplace bullying. While she spoke, everyone else in the room, except for the HR director sitting in the front row, was hoping something would happen to make the presentation come to an end.

Three floors above, an executive-level team reviewed the quarterly reports, looking for ways to improve response time for service outages, especially for customers with any connection to health and welfare activities.

In the other wing of the building, Mary updated her boss's travel schedule. He was leaving in an hour to visit the company's nuclear facility to observe the weekly system performance tests and security evaluations. He was in his office tying up last minute details for the meeting with the board the day after he returned.

Tyler checked the safety strap on his belt harness as he prepared to climb the tower West of the building to troubleshoot a relay and change out a lamp while he was there. He smiled as he heard and felt the hum in the air. Tyler liked to think the tower was a living beast, and the hum was it's breath. The beast was waiting for some poor climber to make a mistake. Tyler smiled and patted one of the tower's massive steel legs. He knew that he did not make mistakes.

Then, the lights went out.

"What the heck is going on?" Mary's boss said as he came out his door holding his dead phone. It was then he noticed the lights. And the silence. Mary said something to him from under her desk where she checked the connections for her computer, but he did not understand her.

A low rumble of laughter swept through the training room when the screen went dark. It slowly turned into louder conversation as everyone realized the screen was not the only thing that was dark.

The executives groaned but kept working so they could complete their review before closing time. One person noticed the clock on the wall had stopped and reached for his phone to check the time. Then he noticed the lights.

The building's electronic alarms remained silent, the emergency lighting remained dark, and the expensive equipment designed to protect the company's sensitive data files from any and all risks, did not.

One hundred and ten feet in the air, Tyler felt a brief wave of warmth pass through his body. He stopped climbing. He felt slightly dizzy. Then he noticed the silence. Tyler reached out a hand and held it against the tower. The beast was dead.

Chapter 52

Daryl slowed down, pulled his truck behind a patch of tall brush beside the gravel road, and got out. He could see the buildings where the snoop had driven too, but there wasn't enough cover to drive any closer without risking being seen. The brush was a good hiding place. Not great, but good.

Daryl had followed her down the sidewalk until she came to the car. As she drove away, Daryl thought he would lose her. But when she pulled into the gas station, he smiled.

"Six minutes," he said. How he knew that was just one of the little bits of behavior he had picked up from his experiences. He turned and ran to where he had left his truck. He was breathing heavily as he unlocked the door and got in.

"You're out of shape, my friend," he said. "You got lazy out there in Kansas."

He turned the corner just as the snoop pulled out of the station and drove West out of town. It was easy to follow at a safe distance until she turned on the gravel road. It had apparently rained recently, so his truck didn't kick up the dust. But when the trees ran out, it was time to walk.

Daryl got the things he needed from his duffel bag and set out. The road was too open, so he moved through the fields, and a few ditches, until he was close enough to see her pull a bag from the car and carry it into the cabin.

"What are you doing, Daryl?" he said.

He still wasn't sure why he was following her, or if there was any valid reason to do it. But there was something. Something that just would not let him stop. That's how it was in Tehran.

The intel had just described their target as male, short, with a long beard and a limp. That had narrowed it down to ten or fifteen thousand people in the city. The team had narrowed it down further, to four or five individuals, but the itching inside Daryl's gut pulled him to someone else. The guy didn't limp, wasn't all that short, and had a nicely trimmed beard. No matter how much his team pressed him, Daryl's stomach pressed harder. Finally, more out of wanting to shut him up and complete their mission, Daryl's team agreed to take the time to check his guy out. They located his home, set up an observation point, and watched for any indication that he might be up to no good. Just as they were packing up and thanking Daryl for the time wasted, the truck pulled up in front of the house and three men climbed out. One had a dog. The dog raised its nose in the air, turned to face the team, and that's when the firefight began. An hour later, as the team waited at their evac location, one-by-one they walked over and rubbed Daryl's itchy stomach. The mission had been accomplished.

Daryl blinked Tehran from his mind and came back to the muddy ditch. He looked at the machine shed he estimated to be about seventy-five yards across the open field. He checked the safety on his weapon and moved further along the ditch until the machine shed was between him and the cabin. He crossed the field and moved through the empty building until he reached the door. He leaned against the wall just inside the door and watched.

Daryl still had no idea what he was watching for, but the itching that was about to drive him up the wall told him that's what he was supposed to be doing.

Chapter 53

"You have to stop this. And stop it now."

"Senator! Like I said earlier, there is no reason for us to argue. That is not why I have called. I want to talk with you in your official capacity as a Senator, to prepare you for what you are going to have to do."

"Have to do what?"

"Senator, I am going to call you tomorrow with information that is going to require immediate action from you and your colleagues. I will explain the steps you must take if you want us to stop what God is doing through us. I will explain…"

"An ultimatum? You're giving me an ultimatum? You don't…"

"Senator, if you convince your colleagues to take the steps that I will explain to you, we will stop our actions, and I assure you that we will use every ounce of our abilities to fully cooperate in helping you bring about the changes that need to be made. However, if you and your colleagues choose to not take the actions immediately, well, let me just say that the things God has done through us so far have been nothing compared to what He will do next."

"Through you? What you are doing isn't…"

"Senator, I realize how difficult it must be to accept what is happening. Remember, I know about your beliefs and plans, and how you thought God would use you and your friends to change this country. It has to be difficult to understand that God chose me instead. Me, the one you called foolish and threw away. But this isn't the first time God has lifted up a fool to destroy a tyrannical oppressor."

"You can't belie…"

"It is you who cannot believe, Senator. You cannot believe what God is doing through us in six days, instead of waiting and putting up with more faithless behavior that has dragged this country to the very gates of hell. You are the one who cannot believe Senator, but I suggest that you spend time in prayer, and pray that God will open your eyes to the truth. Pray that God open your eyes to see what is happening, Senator, and that he will guide you and your colleagues to make the changes I will present. Pray Senator. Pray that your disbelief will be replaced by understanding and acceptance of the one, true, word of God."

Silence.

"Tomorrow, Senator."

Chapter 54

Everything was dark and silent at the corporate headquarters in St.Louis. Crowds of employees gathered in the parking lots as the building was still being evacuated. They compared dead cell phones and told stories about where they were when everything stopped. Some went to their cars, and everyone was puzzled why some vehicles would start, while others would not.

Inside the building, responders worked to free those trapped in elevators and evaluated those experiencing panic attacks. There had been no reports of more serious injuries. The company's disaster readiness team gathered at the building's main entrance and coordinated with the commanders of the various responders. The company's top execs stood in the lobby and made a list of the things they knew were happening out in the service area, and how they were going to deal with them. Their collection of assistants stood next to them using borrowed phones to connect with the locations most likely have problems because of the loss of their connection with corporate.

"Well, at least we have planned for something like this," an exec said. "As long as everyone follows the protocols, things should stay within the safe parameters."

"We sure as hell better hope so," another exec said.

The loss of a signal from corporate set-off a chain of automatic responses. Many of those automatic responses required power to operate. That was why the money was spent to install the array of emergency power supply units in the basement. Those units were on a completely separate network from everything else, so if the normal power infrastructure was taken out for some reason, the backup system would be unharmed and take over. The system was not powerful enough to keep everything at full capacity, but would provide enough electricity to give the company's many facilities and services the time to safely shut-down their systems and avoid any damages.

"The backup system is dead," the man said as he walked up to the group of execs in the lobby.

The alarm system in the corporate headquarters building was dead. However, the one at the power generation facility at the dam one hundred miles to the East was working just fine. As was the system at the nuclear-powered facility up North. It was the same at the seven natural gas pumping stations, and dozens of other company facilities throughout Missouri and Illinois.

In the parking lot, someone shouted.

"Hey, up there, on the tower, is that a person hanging up there?"

Chapter 55

After putting the box back in the drawer, Emily spent a couple of hours cleaning the kitchen. Dad liked to cook but wasn't that concerned about cleaning up afterward. "Hell, if you need a cup, rinse it out. The hot coffee will kill whatever's growing inside it." She straightened up his bedroom, the living room, and finally the bathroom. Anything to avoid thinking. She popped a bag of microwave popcorn, curled up in a chair in the living room, and started thinking again.

"Dammit!" she said.

She felt the vibration from her phone. She wasn't in the mood to answer it.

The vibration stopped, only to start again. Emily took a breath, wiped her eyes, and picked it up.

"Graham," she said.

"Emily, this is Angelique. From Nawlins'"

"Yes, Angelique. What can I…"

"You are in danger, Emily. There is a shadow, a very dark shadow…"

"Yes," Emily said. "I know. I've already taken…"

"Emily, I realize the things I do are kind of unusual, and things like shadows don't make sense to most people. But…"

"No, it's not that. Not at all. It's just that I was already warned, and I've gone someplace out…"

"Emily, wherever you are, you are not safe from this. It is already close, very close. Right now, Emily. It is there this very moment."

Emily felt the shiver as she put down the phone. And then she felt the anger.

"Son of a bitch!" she said as she stomped across the room. "I am sick and tired of putting up with other people's crap. Do this, don't do that, don't speak up, behave, be a good girl, be a good agent, go run and hide. Son of a bitch, I've had enough."

She took a breath. She walked through the cabin and turned off the lights and went to her room to go to bed. She waited until her eyes adjusted to the darkness. She opened the door, went to her dad's room, opened the drawer, picked up the gun, and went back to her room. Then she did something she hadn't done since high school. She quietly slid open her bedroom window and looked out. The tree branch was still there, but it sure looked a lot higher up than she remembered.

"I must have been nuts!" she said to herself as she stepped through the window. But this time, instead of meeting the gang, she was out to deal with her shadow.

Daryl went out the back of the machine shed, and slowly moved to the side of the cabin. He stopped and listened. He moved along the side of the cabin, looking for any other ways in or out, or anything else that might help get his stomach to ease-up. He noticed the little wooden door in the foundation and stopped to get a closer look. That's when she saw him.

She wasn't that high up in the tree, but he was focused on the cabin. As he moved closer, she thought about her options.

"I could wait until he moves past me and then climb down and surprise him from behind."

"I could tuck behind the trunk right here and hold him at gunpoint while I call for help."

"I could just shoot him and ask questions later."

He moved until he was directly below her.

"I could..."

The frustration took over, and she jumped.

Chapter 56

"It's just a short visit," Klass said. "But I will be back again tomorrow when I call the Senator."

"Do you really think he will do it," Ethan Landry said. "Or will we need to go ahead with the next steps?"

"Knowing Arthur, I imagine he will need some additional convincing, but I don't believe he is stupid enough to force us to go that far. Besides, he agrees with what we are wanting to do, he just doesn't like how we are doing it. But even the Senator cannot stop the hand of God."

"Do you want to meet with everyone," Ethan said. "Tonight I mean?"

"No, we'll do that when I get back tomorrow. Is everyone here already?"

"Yes. I was the last one to get here today."

"And how are things at the caves? Having any problems with the devices, or getting them moved?"

"No," Ethan said. "Once we found the problem with the configuration, the devices have worked just as we hoped. And the trucks have had no problems at all. Keeping them hidden in the trailers until they are close to the targets was a good idea. Even if they do try to trace them, they won't point to the caverns."

"What if they figure out how we get them to the unloading location?"

"The trucks take different routes each time, and always end up in the hills down there, in and out of cover. I don't know how in the world they would follow them, even with their satellites. And once you get down in that part of the state they don't have all of those cameras they have everywhere else. I don't think we have much to worry about."

"Good," Klass said.

"And, even if they did find us, Ethan said, "we will see them coming, and besides, there isn't much they can do to us back in those caves like we are. What are they gonna' do, drop a nuke on us? Not with the Missouri tourist stuff that close by. Don't worry."

"I'm not worried," Klass said. "After all, we only have a few more of them to move from there. And if they do force us to take the next steps, the caves aren't involved. Let 'em have 'em."

"Is my wife here yet?" Klass said.

"No, she said she was delayed in Chicago and will be here in the morning."

"Ok," Klass said. "I'm going to get some rest. I have to be at the plane early tomorrow. And, do me a favor. On your way out, tell Wayne to send up one of the girls."

Chapter 57

Daryl felt something.

Maybe it was all the missions, or maybe it was something about the physics of air motion in front of a moving object, but something caused Daryl to jerk his body to the side just before he was hit. The force still knocked him off-balance and sent him rolling to the ground.

She saw him jerk, and she adjusted her feet to make sure they still made solid contact. But moving them meant she was no longer landing in straight form. When she struck, the impact pushed her sideways, and instead of getting her arms wrapped around his neck she tightened her grip on the gun as she rolled across the grass.

Daryl automatically reached for his sidearm and rolled into a firing position.

Emily did the same.

"DROP IT ASSHOLE!" Emily said in a voice fueled by frustration.

"YOU DROP IT!" Daryl said, targeting the spot on the bridge of her nose.

They stared at each other.

"Look," Daryl said, "I'm not kidding here, put down the weapon. I will count to three."

"I'm not even gonna' count," Emily said.

They stared at each other.

"Just who the hell are you, anyway?" Emily said. "And what are you doing out here."

"I can ask the same question," Daryl said. "And what were you doing snooping around in town?"

They stared.

They both realized that the other hadn't shot yet, and took a breath.

"Look," Daryl said. "I'm going to stand up, okay? I'm just going to stand up. Nothing else. Okay?"

"Nothing else!" Emily said. "Then you're gonna tell me what the hell you're doing here."

Daryl shifted his weight to his elbows and knees, keeping his eyes and his weapon on her nose. He let out a little grunt as he pushed himself to his knees, and then stood.

"You ought to get up too," Daryl said. "The grass is kinda' wet."

Emily the 357 aimed at Daryl's head as she stood.

"My hat," Daryl said. "I'm going to get my hat."

He kept his eyes on her as he bent to the ground, picked up his hat, and put it on his head.

"You?" Emily said. "You sure picked the wrong getup to sneak around in Cowboy! Who you trying to be, anyway, some wild west, gunfightin', sheriff or something? Where's your badge, lawman? I'll bet it's even got some bullet dents on it, doesn't it? Probably put them there yourself, didn't you?"

"Did anyone ever tell you that you talk too much?" Daryl said. "Just drop the gun before I…"

"Before you what? Gonna whistle and call your horse over here so you can jump on it and ride off wavin' that hat in the air?"

"Jesus!" Daryl said. "I think I'll shoot you just to shut you up!"

They both heard it at the same time. Gravel was being thrown in the air from something coming down the road. Coming fast. They held their guns in place and turned just enough to see the car slide to a stop in the yard. The door opened, and a man got out.

Chapter 58

"Looks like I got here in the middle of something."

"Reyes!" Emily said. "What the hell? Here, get this asshole's gun. I caught him crawling around out here doing hell knows what. Get it before I shoot him."

"Okay, hang on, nobody needs to shoot anybody right now," Reyes said. "Now, lower the weapons. Both of you."

Both Emily and Daryl hesitated to make sure the other put their gun down first.

"NOW!" Reyes said.

The guns were lowered, slowly.

"Okay," Reyes said. "Now, Emily, what did you say was going on?"

"I was in the house. I came out here because Steve told me someone was following me and I needed to hide. Someone dangerous, he said. So, I'm sitting in there and Angelique called and told me my shadow was really close. So, I got my dad's old gun, crawled out the window into the tree up there, and that's when I saw this asshole crawling around the house. So I jumped on him."

Lance Reyes just looked at her.

"Okay," Reyes said. "I have a few questions about that, but we'll hold them for later."

Reyes turned to get a better look at the face under the cowboy hat.

"So, what is your version of the story Tex? I hope it is as interesting as Graham's."

Daryl looked at Reyes, then at Emily.

"Wait," Reyes said as he moved again. "Wait just a minute here. Don't I know you?"

"Just take his gun, Reyes," Emily said. "You two can introduce yourselves later."

"Yeah," Reyes said as the smile appeared on his face. "Shit, yeah! Daryl. Daryl Krebel, the man with the magic stomach! My god, man. How the hell are you? I thought you were dead. Where the hell have you been keeping yourself?"

The two men shook hands, patted backs, punched arms, and Reyes patted Daryl's stomach.

"Been in Kansas since I got out," Daryl said. "Things had changed in the outfit, and you know I was never all that good at dealing all that well with all those new rules."

"Hell yeah. My god, man. Remember that night in, what was it, El Salvador? Those guys in the three armored trucks? Jesus, that was a night! Kansas? What the hell you been doing in Kansas?"

"It was Managua, not El Salvador," Daryl said. "The trucks I mean. El Salvador was the bulldozer and the busload of strippers. But, yeah, hell of a night. And Kansas? Well, I've been working as a sheriff out there, not too far from Wichita. Wanted someplace quiet. Looks like you're still wearing the uniform? Probably got a bunch more ribbons on it too?"

"Me," Reyes said. "Yeah, kind of. But not with the old outfit. We're doing some new things, a few things not in the usual advertising brochure, if you know what I mean?"

"Sounds like you," Daryl said.

"Damn! Have you heard from any of the other guys," Reyes said. "Like Ritchie, maybe, or Whizbang? I lost track of them when the unit was broken-up. My god man, it's good to see you."

"You too, Willy," Daryl said. "I can't believe it's been…"

The gunshot shattered the air, sent the Starlings screeching into the sky from the tree, bounced off the machine shed and echoed four or five times in the distance.

Reyes jumped and turned to see Emily smiling.

"Hi there," she said. "Remember me?"

"Shit!" Reyes said, "Graham, what the hell are you trying to do, give me a heart attack?"

"I hated to break up your little family reunion," Emily said, "but would one of you lovebirds care to tell me what the hell is going on here? Why is your poorly costumed pal here in the first place, and you? What the hell are you doing here too? And, I guess while you're at it, how many more are scheduled to end up here tonight? Maybe I should go inside and throw together some sandwiches and ice down some beer or something?"

"You apparently know her," Daryl said. "Does she always talk this much?"

Emily raised her gun. Reyes stepped between them.

"Okay," Reyes said. "Okay, put it down. I'm sorry. The man in the white hat used to be one of the best black ops in the business…"

"The best, you meant to say?" Daryl smiled.

"And the most humble guy you could ever meet," Reyes said.

"Yeah, I got that part," Emily said. "I'll bake cookies for the reunion later. Right now I want to know why the hell Mr. Black ops and you are here. How the hell did you even know where I was?"

"I'm here because we got the message you were in trouble," Daryl said. "I was already in the area, so when Chambers called, we decided I was the quickest response. So, here I am."

"Keep going," Emily said. "How did you know where I was. And, now that we're going, that message saying I was in trouble, where did that come from? And if your buddy here is the big danger, you might want to tell them to look closer before they call out the troops."

Reyes glanced at Daryl.

"Amazing!" Daryl said. "You want to shoot her? Here, take my gun."

"Just stop it, both of you," Reyes said. "I don't know why Daryl is here, but we're certainly going to find that out shortly. As for your other questions, Chambers said he got a call from some Senator's office. And I knew where you were because we've been tracking you. Any more questions before we hear from Daryl?"

"Tracking me? Who has been tracking me? And how? It's not my phone. Liz told me…"

"No, it's not your phone. Your friends Liz and Angelique set it up."

"Liz and…" Emily stopped. Her mouth stayed open as she stared at Reyes.

"Hey, nice job," Daryl said. "You found the off switch. I hope you remember how you did it. We might need it again later."

"Graham, while you search for your next sentence," Reyes said, "let's have Daryl here tell us his story."

"Yeah," Daryl said, "okay. Like I said, I was in Kansas, doing the Sheriff thing. Then we had that thing in Lindell, and all the uniforms came in. It just…"

"Lindell," Reyes said. "You mean the EMP attack."

"Yeah," Daryl said. "Those were thirty-nine of my people. But then the uniforms came in and made it clear that I was going to have nothing to do with it all, and that just pissed me off. Then I heard about the attack in Springfield, and, well. I got in my truck."

"But why are you here?" Emily said. "Out here? What's that all about?"

"I was in town there, looking around," Daryl said. "And I saw you snooping around, pretending to be some kind of reporter or something. I knew something wasn't right. One tip for the future. If you're going to carry a notebook around like a reporter? Remember to stop and write something in it once in a while. Just a suggestion for…"

"You came out here and almost shot me because I didn't write in my notebook?"

"No, I came out here because you were snooping around. I almost shot you because you jumped on top of me from that tree."

"You were the one snooping around. You and that stupid hat. And you were…"

"Ok, ok," Reyes said. "So, what it comes down to is that you two both ended up in Springfield to check out the attack, and then Graham, you saw Daryl in his hat and assumed he was up to something. And Daryl, you chased Graham down because she didn't write in her little notebook. Then you both came out here and ended up standing in the dark pointing guns at each other. Have I got that about right now, you two?"

"Well, it's not…" Daryl said.

"God," Reyes said, "I can't wait to tell Chambers about this. He's going to have…"

Reyes heard his phone and pulled it from his pocket.

"Well, speak of the devil," Reyes said as he answered.

"Yeah?" Reyes said. "Okay. St. Louis? When? Two? Should be just over an hour or so. Yeah. I'm on it."

"What was that all about?" Emily said.

"There has been an attack in St. Louis," Reyes said. "Two of them. I need to get down there."

Reyes looked at Daryl.

"You want to ride along?" Reyes said. "Or do you have any more reporters to chase down?"

"Yeah, might as well," Daryl said.

"We'll take my car," Reyes said. "Tanks full."

"I need to do something with my truck."

"Just leave it here. If that's okay with you, Graham?"

"Twenty-five bucks a day, plus tax," Emily said.

"Graham," Reyes, said.

"Yeah, okay, fine. Just don't park it on the grass."

"You coming too?" Reyes said as he looked at Emily.

"No, not now. As much as I would enjoy sitting in a car listening to your war stories, I have something I need to do first, I'll get with you later."

134

"Okay, Chambers will know where we are," Reyes said.

"Hey!" Emily said, "Before you go, that thing you said about Liz and Angelique helping you track me here? You care to explain that, please?"

"Don't know," Chambers just said they had put it together and could see where you were. That's all I know. Really. Now, we gotta go."

Emily watched the car drive down the road as she pressed the number on her phone.

"Chambers."

"Colonel Chambers, it's Emily Graham."

"Graham, are you all right? Is everything okay?"

"Yes, Colonel. I'm fine. I'm sure your buddy Reyes will tell you all about it. But, just keep in mind that he is probably going to make up a bunch of stuff to make it sound more interesting."

"I don't underst…"

"Colonel, I have a favor to ask, and I'm not sure if you can do it or not."

"What is it?"

"Is there any way you can get me on a plane to D. C.? Either tonight or first thing in the morning? It's important."

"D. C.?" Chambers said. "Where are you?"

"Illinois. Springfield. Right where you told Reyes to find me."

"Yeah, okay. Just a minute."

Emily heard him talking to someone.

"Graham? We have a little plane on its way from Chicago now. It will be at the Springfield airport in thirty minutes. Will that work?"

"I'm on my way. Thanks, Colonel."

"Want to tell me anything about the reason for this trip, Graham?"

"I think we both know, Colonel. But I'll fill you in later. Thanks again."

Emily felt the vibration as she put her phone in her pocket.

"Graham," she said.

"Emily, it's Reyes. You know that danger they talked about when they told you to go out to your cabin? I just wanted to say that I don't think they were talking about Daryl. Watch your back, okay?"

Chapter 59

Emily pulled into the airport parking lot at the same time she realized Chambers hadn't told her where to meet the plane. She figured it couldn't be that difficult to find this late at night, so she found a spot in long term parking and walked toward the terminal.

As she crossed the lot, she noticed the line of small planes sitting together North of the terminal, so she decided to start looking in that direction. She approached a man in an orange vest standing next to a very expensive looking jet.

"Excuse me," she said, "I'm looking for a small plane coming to pick me up. They said it was coming from Chicago. It's probably military."

The man looked at her.

"Are you Emily Graham?" he said.

"Yes," Emily said.

"This is it then. It just landed."

"This?" she said. "When they told me it would be a small plane, I was expecting something a little different than this."

"Yeah," he said. "It's really something isn't it?"

"Sure is," Emily said.

"We don't see many like this around here," he said. "But this is the second fancy one we've had since yesterday. It's really unusual."

A man in uniform stepped from the door of the jet.

"Emily Graham?" he said.

"Yes, that's me."

"Come aboard, ma'am. We're ready to go."

Emily started up the small steps and stopped. She turned and walked back to the man in the brightly colored vest.

"Ma'am?" the uniform in the door said. "Ms. Graham, we are ready to take off. You need to come aboard, ma'am."

"This is the second one?" she said to the man.

"Yeah, but the one yesterday was even fancier. Must have cost a fortune."

"When was it here?"

"Well, it landed around eight in the morning. It was only here for a short time, less than an hour. I wanted to get a better look at it, but…"

"Can you tell me anything about it? What kind it was, Numbers, anything like that?"

"I can do better than that," he said. "I took pictures. On my phone."

"Here is my email," Emily said as she handed him her card. "Would you please send me one of those photos?"

"You bet. I'll send them as soon as I'm finished getting this one out. I think they are waiting for you."

Emily walked up the steps and settled into one of the overstuffed seats.

"I'm sorry," she said to the man in uniform. "I needed to…"

"No problem, ma'am. The Colonel just told us to expedite things."

"Yes, thanks," Emily said. "I'll behave from here on."

"Make yourself comfortable, ma'am," he said. "Is there anything you need before we take off? Something to drink, maybe?"

"Uh, no. No thank you," Emily said.

"We will be airborne in about five minutes, ma'am," he said. "And, uh, if you need a restroom or anything, it's back there, through that door."

"Thank you, I appreciate it," Emily said as she heard the engines spool up.

"We should be on the ground in just over an hour," he said. "The Colonel directed us to take you to Reagan, I hope that fits with your plans."

"That's perfect, yes, thanks."

The man went through the door to the cockpit and she felt the plane begin to roll. She felt the plane leave the ground at the same time she felt the vibration from her phone. She opened her email and scrolled through the pictures that had just arrived. Most were of the plane, but one included a group of people standing nearby. Emily smiled as she recognized one of the men from a newspaper photo. His name was Klass VanHollings.

Emily pressed the number on her phone.

"Chambers."

"Colonel, I wanted to call and thank you for the little plane."

"I thought you might get a kick out it," Chambers said.

"I did. And Colonel, I have something you may get a kick out of as well."

"What's that?"

"I'm going to send you a couple of photos, from Springfield."

"Ok?" he said.

"They are photos of another fancy plane that was in town yesterday."

"Yes?"

"And one of the passengers on that plane was Klass VanHollings."

"VanHollings? He was actually there? You have pictures?"

"Just for a brief time, but it was during the time of the attack. I thought you might be able to use the pictures to get what you needed to trace the plane, and maybe find out where it goes? If he is getting some kick out of being nearby during the attacks, you might be able to use this to find him."

"Send them to me and we'll get on it. If they can help us find that son of a bitch, maybe we can put a stop to this mess."

"You'll have them in the next ten minutes."

"And Graham," Chambers said. "You need to know that the Senator is a powerful man. And I'm not talking about his role on all those committees and stuff. The man has some strange beliefs, and that has put him in with some very dangerous people."

"Colonel, I appreciate it, but I assure you, I do understand what you are saying. The Senator and I have some history. We go way back. In fact, we spent quite a bit of time together several years ago. You might say he had some real influence on my career. That's part of the reason I am making the trip. But thanks, I'll be careful."

Chapter 60

In Springfield, and the two locations in St. Louis, the emergency response vehicles were only outnumbered by those from the media. There were dozens of tents and platforms, all lined with cameras and the glaring lights needed to capture every detail on the face of the next person with the latest, breaking update. Hundreds of people carrying microphones, cameras and lights searched the crowds of gawkers for that next image or story that would be aired, live, to those watching or listening.

In Springfield, the media talked about the power that was slowly being restored to most of the traffic lights and other things around the capitol complex, and the places that would remain dark. They described the lists of successful evacuations, and the impact of the how well most places had implemented the policies they had prepared for such an emergency. The media in Springfield mentioned the work being done to restore most communications systems throughout the region, and the number of places where things were already returning to normal. They spent even more time on the stories about the deaths of those people who could either not call for help, or for whom help could not arrive quickly enough. They showed the same video loops, the same photos, and replayed the same brief clips of people in pain. Lanna Gilbert had already told the story of the elevator and her panic attack on seven television networks, eleven radio stations, and was negotiating appearances on three, national, morning television programs. The short video interview of Kyle Bagshaw, the one shot outside the bar, had gone viral and was up to two million hits. Every media outlet repeatedly asked what type of person could have done something like this, why would they have done it, and why here?

In St. Louis, the media talked about the trains stopped along tracks throughout five states, and the lines of trucks blocking streets because they could not load or unload cargo. They replayed the clips of the ambulances and showed photos of the two mechanics who had been injured when the hydraulic hoist failed. Downtown, the media spent most of their coverage on the dangers facing the dam, and the nuclear plant, and displayed maps showing the areas in Missouri and Illinois that may be in danger. One station focused time on trying to get an interview with the CEO of the company that installed the building's power back-up system, so they could ask him why it had not worked to stop the damage. They all showed the photos and close-up video of the man being slowly lowered from the tower and taken away in the ambulance. They gave hourly updates on his condition, interviewed a range of people who gave their expert opinions on why he was up that tower, what had happened to him, and if he had been involved in the attack.

And in all three locations, the media talked about the vans. No official information had been released about them, or the devices, but various unnamed sources described a range of details about where they had come from, and why. One source said the attacks were carried out by foreign terrorists, while another said they were carried out by a militant anti-vaccination group. A source in Springfield said they were from illegal aliens, while a source in St. Louis said they were caused by aliens from Mars, getting even for our sending robots to annoy them. Photos appeared supposedly showing one of the actual devices, until they were found to be taken in someone's garage.

In both Springfield and St. Louis, the media remembered to mention Lindell.

And, in both cities, the media repeated the same assurances that, no matter how much the attacks had disrupted things, they would not cause the nation to panic, or to ever surrender. They said that attacks like this only made the nation stronger, and more determined to stand for the things it had always stood for. The attackers, whoever they are, may have their moment, but the attacks would fail.

Chapter 61

"You just need to understand," the voice said, "I don't know how much longer I"m going to be able to keep a lid on things around here."

"Listen," Klass said. "Everything is going just as we planned, nothing has changed. Tell them to just look at the news and see for themselves. They just need too…"

"Yeah," the voice said, "that's a big part of what's stirring them up. They have been watching. They see all of the things you are doing with that electrical thing you have. Sure, they look big, but they aren't really doing that much damage, you know? You're disrupting some things, yes, but most of them will be fixed up and forgotten about in a couple of weeks."

"That's because…"

"My people want change, Klass. They have been waiting for a long time, and they believed you were finally going to make things happen. Remember, Klass, you and I both know that while these people have many of the same beliefs you and I have, most of them don't think as logically about things as we do. They make their decisions on emotion, and that's all. How the hell else would we have been able to get them to follow like they have? We played with their emotions to do that. I'm not saying they are stupid. Many of them are very intelligent people. But they run on pure emotion. They don't want to think, and they don't trust anyone who does."

"They have too…"

"No," the voice said. "That's just it. They don't 'have' to do anything. They're going to do whatever they feel is the best thing to do. And right now, they want to forget about your plan and start tearing things up."

"That would…"

"I know what it would do. And I also know my people aren't the only ones feeling that way. Klass, I've heard that a couple of groups have already decided to start doing things on their own. I'm trying to find out who they are and calm them down, but I'm afraid we may see some things get out of control in a few places, and soon."

"You need to find out who it is, and stop them," Klass said. "Just remind them what is really going on. We aren't doing this to destroy everyone. We are doing this to convince them to surrender and take the steps to recreate this nation following God's word. And it will work. We shut down one entire state government. We stopped the transportation and power industry in the entire MidWest. And tomorrow we will..."

"That's just it, Klass," the voice said. "Like I said, you haven't stopped anything. Sure, you've screwed with their schedules and damaged some of their infrastructure, but they're going to fix that. Nothing has been stopped. The same people are still there, and they are going to keep doing the same things they did before. Honestly, the only thing my people have gotten excited about was when you killed those seventeen people in Kansas. In fact, lot of them are walking around wearing hats with the number seventeen on them."

"You are saying that they want to see bloodshed?" Klass said. "You know that was never a part of the plan. What happened in Kansas was a tragic accident. It was a mistake I will bear the guilt of, and I pray every day that God will forgive me. God's rules of war do not call for shedding the blood of innocent people, and definitely not women and children. Even the men, we give them the opportunity to surrender and join the faithful first. Only those who are given that chance and refuse, those are the ones whose blood will flow. Remind them of that. The Biblical rules of war say we do not kill productive citizens, and we do not destroy the very infrastructure we will need to rebuild things after the war. The rules say..."

"Klass, we all know what the rules say," the voice said. "But, rules are for thinking people, Klass, and these people don't want to think. They want to act. And I'm afraid that's exactly what they are going to do."

"So, what are you saying?"

"I am saying you need to do something to show these people that you are leading them where they want to go. You need to show them that, if they wait like you have asked them too, you will give them what they are after. You need to show them it is worth waiting. And you need to show them in a way they won't have to think about."

Silence.

"You know," the voice said. "It might even help if you had one of the attacks target one of the things these people really want to go after. You, know, maybe an abortion clinic, or something with the gays? Those are part of the rules of war, too."

Silence.

"Klass, do you understand what I am saying?"

"Yes, I understand. And now I want you to understand something. God did not call me to make changes to his holy plans to satisfy those people who did not agree with them. God did not choose me to listen to his holy word and then rewrite it to make sure it sounded right to people who were not willing to listen to what he had to say. You need to understand that God chose me for this role because he knew I was the one person who would hear his word and follow it to do everything he wants done. I am the one God chose, not the people wearing those hats, not the little groups wanting to act on their own, not some politician, and not, my friend, not even you. So, you tell your people that God's plan is moving forward exactly as he ordained it. Tell them that those who are patient, those who obey the word that God gave me to speak to them, those people will share in the spoils when we bring the godless leaders of this nation to their knees. And anyone, and I mean anyone, who chooses to go against that word, will be branding themselves as a friend of the doomed tyrants controlling this nation, and as an enemy to God. You tell them that. Tell them."

"Klass, it's not..."

"TELL THEM!"

"Okay, Klass," the voice said. "I will tell them."

Chapter 62

Emily looked at her phone and put it back in her pocket. She pulled it back out, looked at it again, and pressed the button.

"Yes?"

"You will never guess where I am calling you from," Dasilva said.

"Is that something I should care about?" Emily said.

"I know, and I don't blame you. Dammit Em, I'm calling to say how much I hate this shit going on, and that I want to find some way to make it up to you. If you will let me."

"Ok, thanks."

"Em, really. I don't blame you at all, and I'm honestly surprised you even answered. I rode around in a taxi for an hour to find a phone booth. It took that long to find one that actually worked. Can you believe it? We finally found this one outside a gas station somewhere on the other side of Lake Pontchartrain. And in this one, I'm standing in something I don't even want to think about."

"Ok, I give up. Why a phone booth."

"Em, what happened to you is just a piece of something. I don't know what, but I do know that they're listing to our phones, tracking them, following our cars, reading our mail. Hell, I've got them following me. They're following all of us."

"Who is listening and following?"

"That's just it," Dasilva said. "We don't know who, but we do know that some of them are inside and some are outside."

"The agency?"

"Yeah. It stinks Em. And people are being singled-out, just like you were. Some are just grilled for several hours and then warned, others have been put out like you were, and some, well, some of them have been taken away."

"Away where?"

"That's what we'd like to know."

"I'm not sure I…"

"Em, I just wanted to let you know that I'm sorry. The day before you were, well, you know. The day before that, I was called into a meeting and put through the mill. They asked questions about you, everyone involved in the boat thing, and the hacking thing."

"What were they after?"

"Hell if I know. After four or five hours of that, they handed me a piece of paper and told me to sign it. It was a made-up report about you they used to help get you out. They said if I didn't sign it..."

"They'd throw you out," Emily said.

"No. I would never have signed that. They started talking about my family. My wife and kids. My kids Em! They had pictures. They...well, so I signed it. Dammit Em, I'm sorry."

Silence.

"Look," Emily said, "you did what you had to do. You have to protect your family. Forget about it. I'm beginning to think you did me a favor anyway."

"But..."

"No, just forget it. But if it bugs you that much, you buy the beer when we get together next time. The good stuff."

"Thanks, Em. I can't tell you how..."

"Arturo, I have a question for you."

"Ok."

"During those hours in that room, did anyone mention anything at all about a senator, or did you see anything that might have had something to do with a senator? Anything at all?"

"No, nothing like that. They talked about what was going to happen to you, and what they would happen to me if I did not go along. They mentioned a few others who had filed things about you, but..."

"Others? Do you remember any of them? Anything about them?"

"The one that seemed to have started it all was a report they showed me from someone back during your training. Someone who said you had done things that violated academy policy and may even have faced federal charges if he hadn't decided to cut you a break. It was from one of the trainers, or someone like that. Do you know what that was all about? I'm guessing they made it up, just like they did the one they made me sign."

"No. No, I'm afraid they didn't make that one up, Arturo. Not now. That one was made up a long time ago. I will tell you all about it over those beers."

"I need to go," Emily said. "We'll talk again one of these days. Take care of yourself, you hear?"

"Yeah, you too Em."

Chapter 63

       The trucks traveled five miles apart, South of Little Rock on Route 30, headed to Texarkana, and then to the warehouse in Alexandra. After unloading, both vans would continue moving South, but one would leave before the other. They needed to reach their locations at the same time and Baton Rouge was about three hours closer than Pascagoula.

Chapter 64

It vibrated again as soon as it was in her pocket.

"Shit!" Emily said.

She pulled it and slapped the button.

"Graham!"

"Thought you would want to know," Chambers said, "we ID'd the plane."

"That was fast! How did…"

"Between the numbers on the plane, a little help from one of our friends, we have the flight records going back a few months, so we can see where they've been hanging out. And, another friend is keeping an eye on where it goes now. In fact, would you like to know where your friend is right this moment?"

"Sure," Emily said. "And if it's along my way I may stop in and say hello."

"Afraid not. Right now it is sitting on the ground just outside of Marion, Illinois."

"Marion? What the hell is it doing down there?"

"We've sent a team to see if we can find out. They'll be on site in about twenty minutes. And we've already started collecting video from any cameras around there. We've not contacted local authorities yet since we don't know who whose side they might be on."

"Colonel," Emily said. "I have to say that I am damn glad I am on your side."

"I could say the same thing, Graham. Can you think of any reason he might be in Marion? Since you're from up in that area, I thought maybe you might know something about the area?"

"I spent most of my time further North, but that area is big for things like hunting and fishing, for people who like to get out and do those kinds of things. Go a little further South and you're in the National Forests, with some great places to wander and get lost. Or hide-out."

"Sounds like we might want to do some looking around out there."

"It's tough, lots of cover. But, yeah. If he was looking for a place to hide and still be within reach of civilization, he could do a lot worse."

"We'll get on it, thanks."

"Colonel, you don't think that's where the next attack is going to take place?"

"No, I don't think so. We're not telling anyone about this yet, but we were able to dig around and identify how those vans got to Springfield and St. Louis."

"Really? That is great!"

"We don't have it all yet. We tracked them to a couple of warehouses outside of St. Louis, that's where they came from. We sent teams there and found the semis that must have brought them there, but they had fake tags and registrations. We've not found out where those came from yet, but we have some…"

"Friends working on it?" Emily said.

"Yes," Chambers said. "You can never have enough friends, you know. This is all between you and me here Graham. Right?"

"Yessir," Emily said. "I appreciate your letting me know."

"By the way," Chambers said, "is that little plane holding up to your standards?"

"There's no pool," Emily said.

"I'll turn in the requisition first thing in the morning. Anything else?"

"Have a nice evening, Colonel."

"You too, Graham."

Chapter 65

Emily put the phone on the table, leaned back in her seat, and closed her eyes. Then she remembered the files Liz had sent earlier. She had forgotten all about them.

She picked up the phone, opened the folder, and began flipping through what was inside. She read about the list of the Senators contributors, official and unofficial. She looked at his emails, including those from the account on the server that, according to his Press Secretary does not now, and never at any previous time did exist. She read the old emails from Berend VanHollings and the more recent ones from Adrianna and Klass. She read those from people from various groups holding a range of nationalistic ideas, some of them you would find on the watch-lists of several federal agencies. She read his schedules, public and private, and was happy to see that he was still planning on being in his office in the morning. She was tired. She decided to open one more file before stopping. It was an older file, written more like a diary than something a Senator would write. It was something he had written long before he was a Senator. Back in the days he did some work with the FBI. Emily read it.

She put the phone down, again, leaned back, again, and closed her eyes, again. The sound of the engines helped her mind drift away. She saw the waves were rolling against the beach as she fell from the top of the tall palm tree. She fell past her mother, sitting in a beach chair and her father standing behind, tying a strand of her hair to a giant gold ring sticking out of the sand. She waved as she fell past Dasilva and his family walking together, picking up shells. She fell past the senator, grinning and holding that piece of paper in his hand. She was still falling as she watched the cowboy coming toward her, riding his horse and waving his big, white, hat in the air and shouting, "Wah Hoo!"

Chapter 66

"Good morning," Chambers said. "I am sorry to call you this early, but it is important. Is everyone on the line? Graham? You here?"

"Yes, I'm here," Emily said.

"Reyes?"

"Here, Colonel," Reyes said. "And Daryl is with me."

"Daryl?" Chamber said. "Who the hell is Daryl? What I have to say is classified, Lance."

"I understand that, Colonel," Reyes said, "and I'll vouch for him. We were in same ops outfits back in the day. Lucky Tummy Krebel, I think you knew him too."

"Yeah, I remember. But I don't understand why he is with you, and why you believe he should be on this call."

"Daryl was the Sheriff in Lindell, Kansas, Colonel," Reyes said. "When he heard about the attack in Springfield he went up to see what he could find out. Graham kind of ran into him and got us together. And, you might remember, he was one of the best for dealing with any kind of electronic stuff, like that thing…"

"The best," they heard Daryl say.

"Yeah, the best at dealing with stuff like that thing we ran into outside of Beirut. He took care of that, remember?"

"Yeah, I remember," Chambers said. "Ok, but what I'm about to tell you all has to stay right here for now, everyone got that?"

"Yessir," three voices said.

"Then listen-up. I told Graham last night that we had been able to trace those vans back to some warehouses around St. Louis, where they unloaded the vans. I can now tell you we've been able to trace the trucks back to an area of Southwest Missouri, about fifty miles South of Springfield."

"That's excellent, Colonel," Emily said.

"Like I said, we traced them to a location somewhere within about a three-mile radius, but we haven't pinpointed their exact location. With the terrain, there are a lot of places to hide down there.

Plus, we have to be careful to not let anyone know we're looking around. Anyone down there might be on their team."

"We'll head that way and help out," Reyes said. "We may be able to..."

"Hold on that, Reyes," Chambers said. "I have more to add. And it's even better. We didn't identify this area until early this morning, but we went back and looked at images from the past 48 hours. Along with identifying the trucks that went to St. Louis, the images showed two more trucks leaving that area late last night, headed South. And then, using the live feeds, we followed them to a warehouse outside Alexandria, Louisiana. Two vans have now left that warehouse."

"Do we know where they are going, Colonel?" Emily said.

"They're still active. One left five hours ago, went past Baton Rouge and New Orleans, and right now is moving East between Gulfport and Biloxi. The second van left about an hour ago following the same route, but just getting to Baton Rouge."

"We aren't going to try and stop them are we, Colonel?" Daryl said.

"No. As much as we would like to, we have to just watch and learn. You know as well as I do that if we take action now, we might avert these two attacks, but Klass and whoever is with him would just disappear until they send the next ones, or worse. Hell, if they are smart, they have some contingency plan to be implemented if we did try to stop them like that. Who knows what the hell that might involve? We need to locate their base of operations, locate Klass and anyone else in some leadership capacity, and take them all at the same time. That's the only safe way to do it."

"What do you want us to do, Colonel?" Reyes said.

"There's one more thing," Chambers said. "And it's the real reason I called you this morning. I just received a message informing me that the satellites we have been using to track the vehicles are being repurposed. They are apparently needed to monitor some type of crisis at the Mexican border, and will be unavailable to us again for at least seventy-two hours."

"Where did..."

"And," Chambers said, "and, more than half of the teams we tasked to locate the base in Missouri are no longer going to be available to us. They are being reallocated to the, uh, crisis as well. You all know very well what I am thinking, don't you?"

"Where is it coming from, Colonel?" Reyes said. "Who is trying to slow things down?"

"All I've been able to find out is that it's high up," Chambers said.

"The Pentagon?" Reyes said.

"They're raising as much hell about it as I'm going to," Chambers said. "It's higher than that."

"So, what do you want us to do, Colonel?" Reyes said again.

"Stay where you are for the moment," Chambers said. "For now, as far as we are concerned, I did not receive the information I just told you about. We are moving forward as planned until, well, we're moving forward. And Reyes, and you Krebel, it may be our good luck that you two ran into each other. I pulled some strings and got Reyes access to get a good look at one of those devices in St. Louis. You're about to get a message with the location, and your identification information."

"Identification?" Reyes said.

"For the rest of the morning Reyes, you are not Colonel Lance Reyes. You are Phillip Wiggins, with the National Science Institute. You are there to evaluate any long-term risks the device may hold."

"Wiggins?" Reyes said.

"And, Krebel, it will take us a few minutes since we just found out you were there, but, you are now, well, let's call you George Kemper, one of the whizbang brains from the Institute."

"Is that a real thing, Colonel?" Daryl said. "Whizbang, I mean?"

"It is now. And you'll have the papers to prove it. Hell, you two are even on their website. And, congratulations on that paper you just had published. You might want to take a look at it before you go in."

"We'll do that, Colonel," Reyes said.

"And Graham?" Chambers said. "The one thing we have been able to find out is that at least some of the pressure for this reallocation decision came from a committee. We checked. A couple of the members of that committee are Senators. In fact, I believe you may know one of them. I just thought you might want to know that."

"Yessir," Emily said. "Yes, sir I do."

Chapter 67

"That's our exit coming up, sixty-one South."

"Got it."

The van slowed and made the turn from One Ninety into the traffic moving toward downtown Baton Rouge.

"We should see the tanks in just a second or two, there they are. Remember, if anyone stops us, you took a wrong turn somewhere."

"Yeah. There's the road. How do you pronounce that anyway? G, S, U? G'soo, something like that?"

The van turned on Gsu Rd.

"It's the first left. Not the one with the gate. There, the next one. See it?"

"I just don't understand that. Every entrance into this place has some kind of gate, or guard shack, or something. Except this one. What's with that? I don't get it."

"Here it is. Take it kind of slow, like maybe we're not sure which way we want to go. Just in case someone sees us."

The van turned left from Gsu, and traveled the half-mile between the rows of storage tanks.

"Here's the parking lot. Pull in that driveway and stop where it circles around. I'll get the thing armed."

The two men walked to the parking lot on the other side of the refinery's business office building and got in the car as the jet taxied to a stop just three miles to the North.

Klass sat on the side of the bed and put on his shoes. "You get out here," he said to the woman as he left the room. He stepped down onto the airport tarmac where the group was waiting. They joined hands and prayed. Klass turned to face the South as he raised his arms in the air.

Chapter 68

"Good morning, Grandpa," Ronnie said as he sat down. Grandpa smiled.

"I am glad you came back this morning, Ronnie. Very glad." Ronnie returned the smile.

"I promised I would listen to everything. So I will. I owe you that."

"Thank you. Where do we begin this morning?"

"I have more questions about yesterday, but maybe we should talk about other things first so we make sure everything is taken care of. I don't know where all this is going to end up for me, but while I am here I will do the job you asked me to do."

"Good," Grandpa said. "You know about the problems last night?"

"Yes. Do you think its part of the next phase of..."

"No," Grandpa said. "It was just in one or two places down South, so I think it was most likely the work of some of the other groups with similar ideas. You know, when one of those groups gets in the news, others always follow."

"That means there will probably be more if we aren't able to stop things soon."

"Yes," Grandpa said. "That's exactly what it means. So we need to find a way to bring this situation to a close quickly, and in a way that will cause those other groups to take a step back from the brink."

"And we have to do it even with the Senator and his people interfering. They are the ones who have forced some of our usual sources to stop helping, aren't they?"

"Yes," Grandpa said. "But remember Ronnie, Senator Murena is not our real problem. People like the Senator are never the real cause of the things we have to deal with. Politicians, and the others that everyone sees as the 'rich and powerful', stay rich and powerful only as long as they do the bidding of the people who created them. If they ever refuse to do what they are told, their powerful role, and sometimes their lives, can come to a very sudden end. We will watch the Senator, for certain, but only because he may give us what we need to deal with the people with the real power."

"The VanHollings group?" Ronnie said.

"Yes, though I'm not sure how much longer we can call it that. They seem to be even more unsettled than before."

"Yes," Ronnie said. "Good. That might help us…"

"No, not good," Grandpa said. "It means they are less able to keep control of the things they have started. Klass VanHollings would have never gotten this far with his actions if the group was not so unsettled. The group was dangerous when they were united. But like this? The danger is almost beyond belief. As difficult as it is for me to say this, I think one of the things we have to do is find a way to help that group regain their strength. But, for now, what else do we need to talk about?"

"Graham is in Washington. It looks like she is going to confront the Senator about Klass."

"More than Klass, I'm afraid," Grandpa said. "Is someone nearby in case she needs help?"

"Yes. Ever since we learned of the threats the other day."

"Good," Grandpa said, as he reached for his coffee, but stopped.

"What's wrong?" Ronnie said.

"Nothing, just a little dizzy again. I'm fine. It's nothing."

"Your heart again?" Ronnie said. "Have you been back to the doctor about it?"

"It's fine," Grandpa said.

"Grandpa, you really need to…"

"What else do we need to talk about?" Grandpa said. "I understand they have been able to follow those trucks and find out they are coming from?"

"Yes, pretty close at least. They'll have it for sure pretty quick now."

"You know, I am still just amazed at what they are able to do today. I mean, some satellite thing up there miles in the air following cars on the highway. And all those cameras watching license plates and things like that. It's just amazing to me, like one of those science fiction magazines I used to read."

"You were into Sci-Fi?"

"Oh, yeah. Big time. Most of the other guys liked those detective things, but those seemed all the same to me. I think they just read them because of the girls in them. I didn't have anything against girls, mind you, but I thought it was more exciting to fly around the universe fighting space creatures…"

"I had no idea," Ronnie said. "Do you still read them?"

"No," Grandpa said. "But I'll watch a good space movie on TV when I find one."

They drank from their coffee.

"Ok," Grandpa said. "Anything else? And, do you have any more questions for me about what we talked about yesterday? How are you feeling about all that this morning?"

"I'm still thinking it through, Grandpa," Ronnie said. "I do understand why the group does what it does, why it has to do them, but I still wonder if it is really the right thing to do. You know, if it's a good thing to do."

"Sometimes doing right and doing good are tough things to determine, Ronnie."

Grandpa smiled.

"I read that in one of those stories a long time ago," Grandpa said.

The smile eased away.

"Part of the problem with Klass VanHollings, and the Senator and the others, is that they believe they understand what the absolute right and good thing is, for everyone, everywhere. I'm not sure we can ever be that certain in a world this big and diverse. And here, the magic of a country like ours is that everyone has the right to hold their own beliefs as long as they don't limit that freedom for others. Folks like Klass, they don't believe that. They believe that everyone should believe what they do, and that's not democracy. In my mind, their approach is not right, and it's not…it's not good."

Grandpa stopped.

"What?" Ronnie said. "Dizzy again?"

"I'm fine," Grandpa said. "Would you do me a favor and go get me a glass of water? Sammy will get you one."

"Sammy? Who's Sammy?"

"The barista you see every morning. I learned a long time ago that it's always good to know a name when you can. You never know when it might lead to something."

"Yeah," Ronnie said. "I'll get your water."

Ronnie put the cup on the table just as Grandpa was putting something in his pocket.

"What was that?" Ronnie said.

"Nothing," Grandpa said as he put something in his mouth and drank the water."

"You took something. Come on Grandpa, what was it? For your heart?"

"Yeah, just something to calm things down a little bit. Nothing to worry about."

Ronnie looked at his Grandfather.

"And don't give me that look. Your grandmother always did that. I've got a doctor's appointment later this morning."

"Good."

"Yeah," Grandpa said. "He's going to look me over and listen to things and then tell me I need to ease up and remember the things that happen when we get to this age. He'll tell me I need to give up the whiskey and the sex, and that I should…"

"The whiskey?" Ronnie said.

"I mention whiskey and sex and you ask about the whiskey? Really? But, it's no big deal. I have one small glass of whiskey every night while I watch TV. I've done it for fifty years or so, and I really don't think stopping now is the thing that's going to fix me up."

"Ok," Ronnie said. "Tomorrow you need to tell me what the doctor says for real, okay?"

"Okay, but stop worrying," Grandpa said. "If you really need to worry about someone, go make sure someone is keeping an eye on your Emily Graham. Her getting together with Arthur Murena is going to be interesting."

"The Senator?" Ronnie said. "What do you mean?"

"I have a hunch she isn't going there to just talk about Klass VanHollings. Back before he was a Senator, Murena did some things that created some real problems for her. Probably would have cost Graham her career if we hadn't helped. No, I don't think VanHollings is the only thing on her mind, and I don't think the Senator is going to enjoy what is about to happen. So if you want to worry, make it about her."

"I'll check to make sure."

"Well, I need to go get my whiskey lecture. Give the kids a hug for me."

Chapter 69

The refinery stretched almost two miles along the river, so the device in the van was too far away to have any immediate impact on most of the buildings and equipment involved in the actual processing of oil. No one over one thousand feet from the van even noticed when the lights went out in the six large buildings surrounding the driveway where the van was parked. But only a few seconds later, as the signals from the various monitoring and control systems stopped coming from those buildings, the dominoes began to fall.

As at other attacks, while they were well created and tested emergency shut-down procedures in place for every area of the refinery, many of them relied on at least some amount of electricity to trigger them, or to power the opening or closing of pumps, valves, doors, and other components that would bring the refinery to a safe shutdown condition. Batteries had been installed for the most critical of those components, but nothing was there to replace them if they, too, were unusable. As crews became aware of the problems, they rushed to manually open and close those things they could get to quickly enough.

The first pressure release was a small one, but it led to an imbalance in pipeline pressures elsewhere. There was no power for the automatic pressure monitors and adjustment equipment, so a second, larger release of pressure soon followed. And a third. It was that third release that led to the first fire.

One of the men standing near the plane was the first to see the smoke and point it out to Klass.

"Praise the Lord!" Klass said.

Klass shook hands with the men in the group as the car pulled up. A man got out and led a young woman toward the plane, and watched until she went inside. Klass looked again at the growing clouds of black smoke, smiled, and walked up the steps into his plane.

Chapter 70

"I'm sorry," Joslan Nolan said, "but I don't find you on the Senator's schedule this morning, and I am afraid his entire day is full, the entire week, in fact. If you would like to..."

"That's funny," Emily said, "I checked it earlier this morning and he didn't have anything until the eleven o'clock meeting with the group from the Pentagon."

"Uh," Joslan said, "I don't know what you, uh, looked at, um, like you said, but..."

"I'll tell you what," Emily said, "why don't you give the Senator a little buzz there and see if he has a few minutes to talk with me."

"I can't..."

"Just tell him that Emily is here, and would like to talk with him. Tell him I'd like to talk with him about that report he put together for me."

"Report? Which..."

"He'll know which report."

"You know," Joslan said, "why don't I call Ellis Anderson and see if he has a moment to see you. Ellis is the Senator's Communication Director and I'm sure he will..."

Emily glanced at the nameplate on the desk.

"You know, Joslan," Emily said. "I can see that you are very good at what you do here. You are handling me just the way you should handle someone who shows up unannounced like I have. You've been doing this for a while, haven't you?"

"About seven years."

"Wow, that's great. When I talk with the Senator I'm going to tell him how well you have done your job here, and I'm going to tell him he needs to give you a raise. Is that okay with you?"

"Well, yes, of course. But like I said, there isn't any..."

"Hang on a second. I always like to see someone who takes pride in doing their job, you know? I think that's because I'm the same way. When I have a job to do, I'm going to do whatever it takes to do the absolute best job I can do. I think that's how you look at it too, isn't it?"

"Well, yes, but..."

"So, Joslan, I'm here now because I have a job I need to do. And it involves the Senator. So, since we seem to be so much alike, I think you'll understand when I explain that I'm not leaving until you go in there and tell the Senator that Emily is here, and wants to talk with him about that report. You know?"

"Wait here," Joslan said as she stood. "But it won't do any good. And when I come back I'm going to have to ask you to leave, or I will have to call security."

Joslan Nolan knocked on the door to the Senator's private office, opened it, and stepped inside. Less than a minute later the door opened and Joslan came back out.

"The Senator will see you now."

"Thanks, Joslan. And I won't forget about that raise."

Joslan waited until the door closed again, and picked up her phone.

"Clayton," Joslan said. "You need to get in here! And hurry!"

Chapter 71

The van followed Route Ten until it turned onto Route Sixty Three just North of Pascagoula. The road heading South was lined with a collection of warehouses, a refinery, a chemical plant, and a other unmarked facilities, all separated by large spans of bulldozed earth, a landfill, and lagoons filled with what may or may not have been water.

"Any of these places could have worked. I wonder why he didn't pick any of them?"

"I don't know. We just go all the way to the end of the road. Must be some good reason, I guess."

Ten miles to the North, the jet taxied to a stop.

"Stay here," Klass said as he picked up Bible and stepped from the plane. The second plane parked nearby and it's passengers joined Klass as he looked toward the South.

"This one isn't as exciting as Baton Rouge," Klass said. "But it will show them that their entire infrastructure is at risk. It will help convince them to listen to what I am going to say to them."

"When will you tell them?" one of the men asked.

"I'll make the call as soon as we are back in the air."

"And are you still giving them time to decide how they are going to respond?" another man asked.

"One more day," Klass said. "And one more attack. And if we haven't done enough yet to surrender to our demands, tomorrow will do it."

"But what if it doesn't," the first man said.

Klass looked at the man and smiled.

"Then we loose the God's holy hounds of hell."

The van came to a railroad crossing, where the highway stopped. They crossed the track and followed the more narrow road stretching across a mile of marshland. They passed the road leading to the refinery's shipping dock and drove around the big, gray sludge field.

"That looks dead."

"This is what they have done to God's creation. This is why we are here. And look over there at the water toward the gulf. That brown stuff. Yeah, that's why we're here."

They glanced at the car sitting just outside the gate to the flood wall surrounding the facility. There were a half dozen cars in the parking lot in front of the station's metal office building.

"I'll arm it. You pull up next to that building there. It's a small place, so somebody is going to notice the van sitting here pretty quickly, so we need to park and get out of here."

As the two men got into the car outside the gate, Klass ended the prayer, turned, and raised his hands into the air.

Chapter 72

"Come in, Emily!"

"Hello Arthur, it's been a while."

"Yes, it has. And I'm sorry it appears you had a run-in with Joslan. She sometimes tries a little too hard to protect me. With so many people..."

"She's good. I told her she deserves a raise."

"Well, probably so. But she's only been here..."

"Let's come back to that later," Emily said. "We need to talk about other things right now."

"Ah, yes," he said. "I assume you are here about Klass VanHollings and the mess he has created. But I thought you were no longer with the agency. I'm not sure I under..."

"Let's start with that, yes. And, let's begin with how you are involved with it all."

"Me involved? No, no. I have nothing to do with any of what that lunatic is doing. Yes, we did some things together years ago, when his father asked me to help him with that project of theirs. But that ended long before he started any of this stuff."

"But, you knew about his beliefs then? While you worked with him, I mean. His beliefs about the government?"

"Beliefs? I'm not sure if I understand."

Emily smiled and sat down.

"Oh, yes, I'm sorry," the Senator said. "I should have offered you a seat. You just caught me by surprise this morning. Can I get you a drink? Coffee maybe?"

"No, thank you. But you did know about his beliefs?"

There was no knock as the door opened and the man entered.

"Is everything all right Senator? Do you need..."

"No, everything is fine, Clayton," the Senator said. "There was apparently just some misunderstanding about Emily here, everything is fine, thank you."

Clayton Drake looked at Emily.

"Emily," the Senator said. "This is Clayton Drake, my Chief of Staff. Clayton is the one who really runs things around here. And he keeps a close eye on me to make sure I'm doing my job. Like Joslan, he sometimes he may overdo it a bit."

He looks at Clayton.

"Everything is fine," the Senator said. "Go back to whatever you were doing."

Clayton hesitated, then backed out of the room, and closed the door.

"Now," the Senator said. "Where were we?"

"I asked about being aware of VanHollings' beliefs. And, Arthur, remember that you and I spent quite a bit of time talking about your own beliefs some time ago. Okay?"

The senator smiled, walked behind his desk and sat down.

"Okay, sure. Yes, I have never, ever denied or tried to hide the fact that I believe there need to be changes made in this country. That has been a part of my platform since getting into politics. It's no secret that I believe the men who founded this nation envisioned something very different than what it has become. I believe there should be less government control, and that the government has no business doing what it is doing to limit self-determination. And yes, I believe there are some truths that need to be followed. Biblical truths that should guide how a nation operates. But I…"

"And about women."

He smiled.

"Ah, yes," the Senator said. "Now we get to what really bothers you. Yes, I believe in the God-given roles we are meant to play in this world. And those roles are different for men and women. And, yes, before you bring it up, there are other differences. Between our origins, and between cultures that…"

"European-bred, white males are the true leaders," Emily said. "Women and the rest are followers. That's where it leads, isn't it?"

"I didn't make it up, Graham. It's a simple truth. And sometimes the simplest truths are the hardest to accept. But listen. And I want to be very clear about this. I have always believed, and have always made it very clear, that we need to make these changes through the proper channels, working from inside the system to change it. I have never, and will never, support the kinds of actions that VanHollings and the others like him are taking. Those are…"

"But, you do agree with why they are doing those things?" Emily said. "Is that correct?"

"You can agree with what someone believes in without agreeing with things they do," he said as he leaned back in his chair. "And I do NOT agree with..."

"But," Emily stood and walked to look through one of the office windows, "there may be times when you believe it is acceptable to do things outside the system when you believe it is important enough? When there is something you really, really, want? Isn't that right?"

His eyes narrowed.

"That was a long time ago. I was young, and I didn't understand things. I allowed my dedication to blind me to what was right. But that was a long..."

"A long time ago. Yes, Arthur, it was. But, you know, I still remember that morning you called me into your office. I still remember you telling me how grand I was doing, and how, with all of the trainees you had worked with, you had never come across someone with my abilities."

"That was the tru..."

"And, how someone like me could have an amazing future in the agency if I..."

"Listen!" he said. "That was a long..."

"If I would just go along with the work God had called you to do. You called it a mission. A mission from God, that's what you said."

"Graham. This is..."

"You were going to change the world," Emily said, "and I would be..."

"That's ENOUGH!" the senator said as he stood.

"No," Emily said. "There's just one more part. The part about what would happen if I did not go along. The part about the report you created. The report that said I made unacceptable advances to you, had even threatened you, several times. That part, Arthur. That part about the report you presented when I told you to shove it up your ass. That part, Arthur. The part that almost got me thrown out altogether, until they reconsidered and just took me out of the running for the top assignments."

"Ok," the Senator said. "Ok! You've had your say. You had your opportunity to come in here and bitch about something you claim I did a long time ago. But it's over now. You had your bitch-session, but it's over. You have no proof of anything. It's your word against the word of a United States Senator. So, if that's what you came here to..."

Emily sat back down in the chair.

"Arthur, take a breath. Calm down. I didn't come here to bitch at you, although I do have to admit I did enjoy that. I came to say that no matter openly you may admit your personal beliefs and how committed you are to making changes in the right way, I know what you are capable of, Arthur. I know how far you will go to push those beliefs of yours. So, then, when I think about Klass VanHollings, and what he is doing out there, and I think about the connection you have with him, I just have to wonder if there is more going on. And I think about what might happen if people were to find out that a United States Senator was…"

"Alright. Alright," the Senator said as he sat back down behind the desk. "What do you want to know?"

"Are you still connected with Klass VanHollings?"

"Am I helping him do what he is doing now? No. That is the wrong way to make changes and it is going to fail. And when he does it is going to make it almost impossible for the rest of us to talk about those changes."

"Do you communicate with him? Give him…"

"He has called me. I've not tried to talk with him since I threw him out. But, yes, he has called me. Just yesterday. Said he was going to call again today to tell me what this stuff is all about."

"The attacks?" Emily said. "So you did know about them."

"No! I didn't know anything until I saw them in the news, and I didn't know he was involved until he called me yesterday. He's calling me today because I think he believes I will force everyone to give in to his demands."

"What are his demands?"

"I don't know, but I assume they're from his ideas about the holy war he talked about. That's why I threw him…"

"What are you going to do when he calls you with those demands?"

"I don't know," the Senator said. "I am going to…"

"You would like to do it, to force those changes, wouldn't you?"

"I don't know. I mean, this is not how…"

"What I really don't understand, Arthur, is if you know what he is doing is going to create problems for you, why haven't you done something to stop him? I mean, a United States Senator has many ways to…"

"His mother," the Senator said. "As much as I want to…I just can't risk it."

"Adrianna VanHollings? What can't you risk? No, let me guess, she's a major contributor, right?"

"Contributor?" the Senator said. "Adrianna VanHollings is the reason I am in this office."

"She agrees with your beliefs?" Emily said.

"She doesn't care one bit about my beliefs," the Senator said. "She didn't help me get here because of beliefs. She put me here so I could do what needed to be done to protect her interests, plain and simple. You will have a hard time finding anyone in the city that isn't here because of her. Hell, it would be tough to find anyone in any real position of power that she hasn't put there. No, contributors offer money if we do what they ask us too. If we do what Adrianna VanHollings wants, she gives us power."

"So, what..."

"The only way Klass is going to be stopped is to kill him. And if I did anything that led to killing her son, well..."

"Goodbye nice office," Emily said.

"That's not what happens when you cross Adrianna VanHollings."

The door opened after the three knocks.

"The people from the Pentagon are here, Senator," Joslan said. "Should I tell them to wait?"

"No," Emily said. "I think we're done here for now."

"Give me five minutes, Joslan," the Senator said. "Then send them in."

Emily stood, walked to the door, stopped, and turned.

"Senator?" she said.

"Yes?"

"Don't forget about Joslan's raise."

"Yeah," the Senator said. "And Emily, as dangerous as Klass is with what he's doing now, compared to his mother, he's an amateur."

The door closed and the Senator picked up his phone.

"Clayton, I believe its time we did something about Graham."

Chapter 73

"Hey, is your computer still working?" Fred yelled across the room.

"Nope, just went down," Javier said. "Yours too?"

Then they noticed the lights. And the air conditioning.

The seven people at the natural gas terminal this morning began looking for the reason for the loss of electricity. When one of them tried to call the downtown office and realized their phones were dead, they began to realize something bigger had taken place.

"You don't think this is one of those things like in Illinois and Missouri, do you?" Javier said.

"Here?" Fred said. "Why would anybody want to do that here? I mean, we don't even have any unloading going on."

Ten miles North, Klass rubbed his shoulder.

"Now I understand why Aaron and Hur had to help Moses hold his arms up like that," Klass said. "I mean, that went on all day until sundown. Wow!"

Klass noticed one of the men still looking to the South.

"What's up? See something?"

"No," the man said. "I was just wondering."

"What?"

"Well, it seems like the other missions were bigger than this one, had more impact. I'm just wondering why we did this one. I'm not questioning your decision at all, but..."

"Don't worry about it," Klass said. "I understand. There are two reasons we did the terminal here. First, it's part of the infrastructure that people don't think about a lot. So, it will surprise a few of them. The impact isn't fire and smoke, but just the reminder of how vulnerable they really are."

"Yeah, I see."

"And second, it's partly psychological. When they see this one that looks little, they might relax a bit. They might think we've done the worse we're going to do. And, tomorrow, I mean it was already the biggest mission of all, but after this one, it's going to look even that much bigger. We're playing with them a bit."

"That's why God chose you to lead this, I guess. Thanks."

"Let's get going," Klass said. "I have a call to make."

Chapter 74

"Senator," Joslan said as she leaned through the door to the conference room, "I know you said no calls, but it's from 'him' again. Do you want me to…"

"Put him through, Joslan. In my office, please."

The Senator stood and walked to the door.

"I am sorry," he said to the group from the Pentagon. "But, I do need to take this. Why don't we take a brief break."

He closed his office door and picked up the phone.

"Klass, I'm afraid I only have a second here right now. I'm in an important meeting with…"

"No," Klass said. "You listen this time. I talk, you listen."

"Now, just…"

"You don't need to write anything down. A package will arrive there anytime now. But, I'm going to explain things to you now so you can get started. The clock is ticking."

"I don't…"

"First, today you are going to learn about two more demonstrations. These are to give you a clear idea of what we are able to do, where we are able to reach. They are to give just a small idea of what this country will face if it does not surrender."

"SURREN…"

"There will be one more demonstration tomorrow, just in case you need the additional incentive to move things forward. Do you understand so far?"

"What do you mean, surrender? Surrender what?"

"I talk, you listen. Remember? In the package you receive, you will find a detailed list of the terms of the surrender. They are non-negotiable and are to be acted upon immediately. Do you understand?"

"You are telling me, what? That you expect this government to surrender to you and your acts of war? And, am I correct in thinking that you expect me to help bring that surrender about? I'm afraid you are very mist…"

"The terms are clear, and call for changes to be made to the U. S. Constitution. The procedures for making such changes are already in place, and I am sure you know how they work."

Silence.

"These are the changes that will be included in the amendments: One, abortion in any form, for any reason, will not be allowed in this country. Two, marriage will be between a man and a woman only, and any existing marriages other than between a man and a woman will become null and void. Three..."

"You can't actually expect that..."

"Three, any and all practices of idolatry or occultism will be illegal. Four, any and all communist behaviors or actions will be illegal. Five, a complete review of all other laws and government policies and actions will be reviewed and amended to bring them in line with Biblical Law. Do you understand the five terms of surrender, Senator?"

Silence.

"Senator, do you understand?"

"Klass, even if I agree with what you are hoping to do, this is not the way to get it done. This country will never surrender, to these or any demands. They will fight. They will hunt you and your people down, Klass. In fact, one of them was just here this morning asking what I knew about what you were doing. They were..."

"Who was there?" Klass said.

"Graham, the one that used to be with the F.B.I. I don't know who she is working for now. But there's nothing to worry about, I've taken steps too..."

"No!" Klass said. "Leave her alone. Graham is the least of your concerns right now."

"As long as you realize that..."

"Those are the terms, Senator," Klass said. "You will take those to the people you know need to hear them, and together you will take the steps to make the changes."

"You make it sound like that is an easy thing to do!" the Senator said. "Hell, I've been working at this for fifteen years now, even trying to make some of the same changes. It takes time. You can't..."

"As I said, there will be one more demonstration tomorrow. If the actions are not begun within twenty-four hours after that demonstration, we will view that as a refusal to surrender, and act accordingly."

"Just what does that mean?"

"This is God's War, Senator, and God's rules of war will be followed. According to those rules, no man's blood shall be shed until he has been given the opportunity to surrender and join us. Any man who refuses to surrender will be destroyed. Any man, Senator. And after twenty-four hours we will begin with those who are leading the tyranny now being imposed on the people of God."

"You are threatening to murder…"

"Assassination to remove tyrants is not murder, Senator. It is God's justice. Those leading the tyranny are nothing more than a band of robbers who will be made to pay for what they have done."

"Klass, this is…"

"Enough, Senator. You have the terms, and you know what you must do. There is nothing more for us to discuss."

Senator Arthur Murena stared at his shoes.

He picked up the phone.

"Clayton, forget what I said earlier, about Graham. I need you to call the committee and set up a meeting in my office in thirty minutes, you know the committee I'm talking about. I don't care what they may have planned for the day, tell them I want them here in thirty minutes."

Klass VanHollings smiled as he pressed the number on his phone.

"Listen, are you still following Graham?"

"Yes," the voice said.

"I am on the way to the camp. You know what to do."

Chapter 75

"Graham," Chambers said, "I'm in the middle of something here. What do you need?"

"I'm sorry, Colonel. I'll make it quick, Colonel. Is there any chance I could catch another ride today? I hate to take advantage of..."

"The plane is right where you left it last night. I've told them to stick around and get you wherever you need to go."

"Thanks, Colonel, I appreciate..."

"Sorry, we haven't got the pool installed yet, though."

"I'll suffer through. Thanks again, Colonel."

"Anytime."

Emily walked toward the street to get a taxi when she saw the coffee shop. She flipped through messages as she stood in line. She ordered her coffee and looked around the room as she waited. Scanning faces was a natural behavior now. She usually had a mental database of images to compare to the faces she saw. Her eyes kept returning to one face. She had seen it before, but where? Not at the agency, or the files there. Not from the television, or a movie. He was too old to be from school. She was still searching her brain when she got her drink and walked out the door toward the street. She waved to a taxi when the face attached itself to a body. It was a body sitting on a stool, next to a counter. The counter at the cafe in New Orleans.

"Raul!" Emily said as the taxi pulled up and she opened the door.

"But Adrianna VanHollings' personal bodyguard wasn't in the shop. So why was..."

Emily's body tried to make it's instinctive response to the push, but it had been strong enough to put her off balance and make her fall into the backseat. She planted her arms against the seat and started to push up. She felt the burn from the needle. She felt the taxi lurch forward, and then nothing.

Chapter 76

"Now you listen to me," Adrianna said. "My husband and I spent years helping turn this group into…"

"Mrs. VanHollings, please," Elton Mann said. "We are all aware of the role you and your husband have played in our organization. The simple fact is, however, that it appears you have lost control of your son and his people, and…"

"I told you I was taking care of that."

"That was four days ago," Sebastian Alvarado said. "And since then your son has created a situation that now puts us at extreme risk. We simply cannot sit back any longer and allow it to become even greater."

"It is not going to become any greater," Adrianna said. "I have taken the steps to…"

"Steps like Agent Graham and your Senator Murena?" Hue Shuren said. "From what we have seen they do not appear to be …"

"You have seen?" Adrianna said. "What does that mean? You have been following me? Checking up on me? You don't believe I am doing what I say I am doing? How dare you…"

"Adrianna," Polachev Savelievich said.

"…I have been…"

"Adrianna, please," Polachev said. "In my country, my grandfather used to say that even the greatest king must at last be put to bed with a shovel. It is an old…"

"And what does that mean?" Adrianna said. "Are you telling me that I am old and need to be put…?"

"And another he always said, was, that no matter how hard you try, the bull will never give the milk. What we are saying, Adrianna, is that it appears to us that your two people are like the bull that you want to give you the milk. They will not give it. And, no, you are not old, but perhaps your ways are becoming such. We know what you have done in the past, but today you have made mistakes, and we must take steps to correct them."

Silence.

"This is because of the others, isn't it?" Adrianna said. "It's because of Herzig, Geller, and Conway, isn't it? And my husband. Just remember that every one of you agreed with those decisions. You agreed that changes needed to be made, but I was the only who would…"

"Yes, Adrianna," Farvad Ghazzi said. "We needed change. But you became so focused on those changes that you did not pay attention to what was happening around you. And that is the mistake that must be corrected."

"So, what are you saying?" Adrianna said. "What do you want me to do?"

"Nothing, Adrianna," Elton Mann said. "You do nothing. We will do what must be done to stop this situation before any more damage is done."

"What about Klass?" Adrianna said. "What about my SON?"

"We will do what must be done," Polachev Savelievich said.

"No!" Adrianna said. "I will not sit here and allow you to do anything that may harm my son. I will NEVER allow that to happen. Do you all understand that?"

Silence.

"DO YOU?"

Silence.

"Adrianna," Elton Mann said. "We are sorry. We must do what must be done."

Chapter 77

"He can't be serious," a member of the committee said. "He can't actually expect us to do this, can he? Not really?"

"I'm afraid he does think exactly that," Senator Arthur Murena said. "And he expects us to start doing it within the next two days."

"Or what?" another committee member said.

"He said that if the country fails to accept the terms of surrender, they will begin shedding the blood of those men who are leading this government that is tyrannizing God's people. It's straight from the writings. We've all read it before."

"Yeah," the third committee member said, "but none of us were ever crazy enough to think about actually doing things that way. Doesn't he realize what is going to happen?"

"It's like I told you earlier about him, from back when I had to stop having him around. He started hanging around with some of the more far-out groups. Before long he ended up beginning to believe he was actually the one they were all waiting for. No, I don't think he realizes what is going to happen. I think he believes we are either going to do what he says and surrender this nation, or that God is going to drop down from heaven and lead the march on the capitol building."

"However it ends," the second member said, "it's going to set our work back by decades. If any of us even mention any of the things on that list of conditions, everyone will tie us to this. Do you know how long it will be before we…"

"That's true, but let's keep our focus on the main issue," the Senator said. "What do we do with the demand to surrender? Right now, it looks like we are the only ones who know about it, other than Klass and his people. We need to come up with some kind of response before word gets out and the media is screaming in the hall."

"Someone probably needs to talk with the Speaker," the second member said. "Then the president."

"Senator," Joslan said as she opened the door. "I'm sorry to interrupt, but he is calling for you again. I thought you would want..."

"I'll take it here, Joslan. Thanks."

The phone rang and he picked it up.

"Yes?"

"One thing I failed to mention in our last conversation."

"That was?"

"Three hours after tomorrow's demonstration, I am releasing the information I sent you to the media. I thought you might like to know. Now, I imagine you have a committee to lead, so I'll let you get back to doing that."

The Senator put down the phone.

"What was that about?" the second committee member said.

Senator Arthur Munera let out a breath.

"We, uh," the Senator said, "we, uh, now have less than twenty-four hours before we need that answer for the media."

Chapter 78

The light was too bright, so she raised her hand to block it.

"Tell him she is waking up," a tinny voice said.

She felt someone grip her wrist.

"Pulse is good," the voice said. "Let's help her sit up."

Emily felt the universe spin as the hands lifted her.

"Whoooa," she said.

"You're okay," another voice said. A woman's voice. "Just relax. You are perfectly safe here."

Her eyes would not focus. She thought her mouth felt like she had been keeping putty in it. She thought about the putty she played with as a kid, pressing it against the Sunday comic strip, making the ink stick to the putty so she could stretch in and make the comics take strange shapes. She remembered that time she stretched the comic about the dog. She giggled.

"Come on," the woman's voice said. "Wake up now. He will be here in a minute so you need to wake up."

She felt the damp, cool cloth on her forehead and her eyes began to form the image of a young woman with shoulder-length hair in front of her. The woman smiled.

"There you are," the woman said. "How are you feeling?"

"What happened?" Emily said as the image of the taxi came back, and the shove, and the needle.

"Where is Raul?" she said as her body tensed.

"Who?" the woman said. "There is no Raul here, Emily. Just relax. Klass will be here in just a minute, so you don't have anything to worry about. Nothing at all."

Images and words were racing through her mind, but not in any order that made sense of them. Until she heard his name.

"Where am I?" Emily said.

"Klass will tell you everything in a few…Oh, here he is now."

The woman stood and stepped to the wall as he entered the small room. Emily began to return to the planet.

"Hello, Emily," he said. "It is nice to finally meet you."

"So," Emily said, "I'm thinking you must be Klass? Where am I? And why am I here? What is..."

Klass turned to the woman by the wall.

"Is she okay to get up, walk around?"

"Sure," the woman said. "I think so."

"Let's go for a walk," Klass said as he held a hand out toward Emily. "Let me show you around and answer some of your questions."

Emily looked at the outreached hand, braced both of her hands on the side of the bed, and pushed herself to her feet.

"Hah!" Klass said. "I love that attitude!"

The two of them left the room and as they walked through the house Emily took in as much detail as her mind would let her.

"I really do apologize for how we had to do this," Klass said. "But I didn't know of any other way. I wanted us to meet and talk, but with things as they are, well, I just can't risk letting anyone know where our little camp is here. You understand, I know."

"Camp? What kind of camp?"

"It's part main base for our operations, and part training facility for our men. I will introduce you to some of them in a few minutes. You see, Emily, the things you have seen so far, the things we are doing with our electronic weaponry, those are just the first phase of what God is leading us to do. After the surrender, we will send our armies out into the population."

"Armies?" Emily said.

"It's all according to God's plan for his holy war. I think you will find it fascinating. But we take men, over the age of eighteen and from families with the right backgrounds, and we divide them into the groups that God ordained, and train them to do their work."

"Their work," Emily said. "And that work would be?"

"Yes, it is confusing at first. God's army is not man's army. What our army will do is more like teaching, teaching people how to live their lives as God intends."

"As God intends?"

"For leaders of the nation to lead in God's image, following God's word and commandments. For citizens of the nation to live lives that follow the one, true word of God. But, let me show you around more. We have plenty of time to help you learn about how to follow God's will with us."

"With you?"

"Come on, let me introduce you to some people."

"And, by the way," Klass said, "we had to borrow your phone for a while. We disabled the GPS sensor and did a few other things to make sure it didn't show your location while you're here. But, don't worry. We'll fix it all up and give it back to you in a bit."

Two hours later, they walked back to the house where a table was set with places for two.

"Here," Klass said, "sit down, let's have some lunch while we talk more."

"No, thanks," Emily said. "I don't…"

"Come on," Klass said. "I realize all of this may be a bit much to take in, but that's no reason to not eat, is it? Besides, Grace over there fixed it special, just for you. You don't want to hurt her feelings do you?"

Emily sat. She looked at the plate of food.

"Go ahead," Klass said as he reached across the table, picked a piece of vegetable from her plate, and put it in his mouth. "It's perfectly safe. I assure you that you have nothing to fear from us here today. Nothing at all."

They talked as they ate.

"I guess I'm surprised," Emily said. "It looked like you must have a thousand people out there in your army."

"Five thousand are here right now," Klass said. "There is a lot more going on here than what you could see during our walk. God's forest provides us good cover. There are more at the other camp. You look like you have more questions."

"Why am I here? And why are you taking the risk of bringing me here? Of showing me what you have here? Aren't you worried about…"

"No, I am not worried. For a couple of reasons. First, because we are following the one, true word of God, and that means we are certain to be victorious. But second, even if I were to show you everything here, you don't know where we are. You know there are trees, and hills, but that could be anywhere. Plus, we took your phone and removed the card from it, so it has no idea where it is either. So, no. I am not worried about you being here."

Klass smiled.

"And as for why you are here, that, too, is from God."

Klass leaned his arms on the table and leaned in.

"Emily, God wants you to be a part of his creation, the new nation he chose me to create."

"I don't…"

181

"I realize it is difficult to understand, but it is true. He has given you so many gifts. That attitude you used to put my father in his place that day on the beach, and that made you reject my help standing up today. God gave you that attitude for a reason Emily. And this is that reason."

Emily sat.

"God wants you to join us. He wants you to help me lead everyone into the new world, the new nation. I will lead the men, and you, Emily, God wants you to use that wonderful strength you have to help the women learn how to follow the men into God's new land. You, Emily. God has ordained it."

"You are an absolute idiot. A full-bore, off-the-wall, certified, male, bozo that needs to be put in a box, wrapped tightly with a log chain, and dropped in a deep, dark hole somewhere very far away from everyone else."

That's what went through Emily's mind.

"I think you may have misunderstood what God was saying," she said out loud.

"I do understand, Emily," Klass said as he leaned back. "This is a lot to take in so quickly. But, it's okay. I don't expect you to understand everything right this minute. God wants me to give you some time to think about all of this. We have one more mission tomorrow before we begin the next phase of the war, so we don't have much time, but another day or two will not matter to God. We'll talk again later."

Klass stood. Emily put her arms on the side of the chair and began to stand when she felt the needle. She felt her body slide back down into the chair, as the room began to grow dark.

Chapter 79

"YOU HAVE TO DO SOMETHING!" Adrianna said.

"I told you, Adrianna," the Senator said. "You tell me what to do and I'll do it. Right now we don't know how we are doing to deal with what Klass has done. We may just turn it over to the Pentagon and let them…"

"NO!, you cannot do that. There has to be another solution. You just aren't trying hard enough."

"Hard enough?" the senator said. "Klass told me about this nine hours ago and I've spent the entire time since then with groups trying to find a solution. Not trying hard enough? And before he called me, I had to deal with that Emily Graham again, with all of her…"

"Graham?" Adrianna said. "What did she want? She hasn't done anything about this either. And after she told me she would find a way to stop it."

"She's digging around, but…"

"Arthur, you have let me down. Both you and Graham, you have both let me down."

"I don't…"

"This is simply unacceptable, Arthur. This is not the behavior I expected from you, that you assured me you would give me when I helped you start building that little empire you believe you run now. But you don't, Arthur. You don't run anything. Anytime I choose too, I can pull it all right out from under your feet, Arthur. You remember that as you meet with all of your little groups to talk about finding a solution. And I suggest you stop chasing that little secretary of yours around her desk and spend that time finding a way to stop what is happening. Do you hear me, Arthur? And if you and the others expect me to sit back here and not do anything to save my son, you are bigger fools than I thought you were."

"Others?" the Senator said. "What others? And I don't expect you to…"

"I don't care what you expect, Arthur, or any of the rest of them. What I care about is that you find a way to fix what is happening."

She paused.

"You'll do that for me," she whispered, "won't you Arthur? After all we have been through together? You'll do that for me, won't you?"

He stared at the phone.

"Arthur?"

"Yes," he said. "Yes, Adrianna, I'll find a way to do that for you."

Chapter 80

"What time did they find her?" Bill Chambers said.

"Around eight o'clock," Lance Reyes said, "we had just landed."

"And she was at the airport?" Chambers said.

"Yeah," Reyes said. "In one of the bars. We saw the EMT's there, and when they rolled by on the way to the ambulance we recognized her. Or Daryl did."

"Okay then," Chambers said. "It's what, eleven now? So, the last time I talked with her was around ten thirty this morning, and she was in D. C., headed back to the plane. Then, some nine hours later, give or take, she turns up in an airport bar back here in New Orleans. So, the question is, where the hell has she been for those nine hours? Do they have any idea how long she's actually been out?"

"Not for sure, but based on what they found in her bloodstream, they're guessing at least maybe three to four hours before we found her. They said it actually looks like she's had two doses of the stuff today, so it may be another hour or two before she comes out of it. She should be fine, but it will take a while."

"Two?" Chambers said. "What's that about?"

"We're hoping she can tell us about that when she wakes up," Reyes said. "Along with a few other things. You made good time, though."

"Yeah," Chambers said, "and that's partly due to Graham too. When she didn't show up at the airport in D.C. I told the crew to bring the jet home for refueling until we found out where she was. It had just gotten back when you called. So, you two got here around eight. Why did you come here? And, did you learn anything in St. Louis? Did you get a look at that device?"

"We came here because of what happened last night," Reyes said. "We're thinking it's related and wanted to see if we could find anything useful. You heard what happened here last night, didn't you?"

"Yeah," Chambers said. "I heard. I'm afraid it was bound to happen."

"And, yes, we saw the device," Reyes said. "Daryl said it looked like one of the early prototypes of the things they were experimenting with several years ago. Right, Daryl?"

"Yeah," Daryl said. "It was one of the first ones that actually put out enough energy to do anything. But the design made it impossible to focus the energy to use as a targeted weapon. It just fried anything within the range you configured it for, just like we've seen. It took another year or two before we had a prototype that could be both configured, and have a focused energy beam."

"Daryl was..." Reyes said.

"Yes," Chambers said, "I know all about Daryl. I took a nice, long look at his record during the flight here. Your friend here wasn't just one of the best ops members..."

"The b..."

"Excuse me," Chambers said. "The best ops team member, he also spent time in a few places that did not exist, working on projects that did not exist. Projects like the device you looked at today."

"He told me about that today when we saw the device," Reyes said. "And, he had an idea that may just help us put an end to the attacks."

"Give me the short version," Chambers said.

"I haven't been involved for a while," Daryl said, "but I know people who still are. And they've told me about the newer versions of the NNEMPs that can be even more narrowly targeted, and mobile. Some of them are the size of a good-sized rifle. The range on them is shorter, but when you can get close enough to the target, they do the job. Of course, if anyone asks, they don't really exist."

"So," Reyes said, "Daryl made a few calls."

"And?" Chambers said.

"And right now," Daryl said, "two of those non-existent devices are sitting on a plane scheduled to land here around midnight tonight. And if you think we can get a bit more information, we have a plan for using them."

"You want to take out the trucks before they get to their targets," Chambers said. "Don't look so surprised. It's the perfect solution. If."

"Yes," Reyes said. "And that takes us to the part about the information we need to know if you can get. Like where Klass is, and where their locations are so we can hit them all at the same time we zap the device."

"Zap?" Chambers said. "Is that the technical term?"

"As a matter of fact, Colonel," Daryl said, "yes it is."

"Well, fortunately, we are now able to track the plane, which is usually where Klass is, and we have located the source of the trucks in Missouri and have teams in position to take it out whenever we give the word. Unfortunately, according to information picked up from our communications people, there is at least one other camp somewhere, a big one. But we have no information about its location. The plane keeps going back to Marion, Illinois, so we assume its somewhere around there. But that's a big area."

"We've not been able to follow them from the airport?" Daryl said.

"Hah," Chambers said. "That's the cute thing about it, about how these people think. We can pick them up leaving the airport, but they always make a stop at a car wash a couple of miles away."

"Car wash?" Reyes said.

"I told you it was cute. It's one of those that your car goes all the way through? And on the days they go there, they have a line of twenty to thirty cars show up at the same time. At some point as the line goes through the building, Klass gets out of one car and gets in another, and then, one at a time, they all come out and head off in that many different directions. We're trying to track all of them, but they know how to use the cover. They do the same thing coming back to the airport. Damndest thing I've ever seen."

The door to the hospital room opened, and Liz stepped in.

"Oh, sorry," Liz said. "I didn't realize you were here talking business. I'd better wait outside."

"No," Chambers said. "Come on in. I'm afraid your as mixed up in all this as we are now. After that thing with the senator's files, I mean."

"Oh, you heard about that?" Liz said.

"Reyes, pull Liz a chair over here so she can join us," Chambers said.

Reyes reached for the chair by the wall and pulled it to him. The chair bumped the bed table and knocked a plastic pitcher to the floor.

"VanHollings," Emily said, "you...crazy...out of..."

"Sounds like somebody else is coming back to join us," Daryl said.

"You...you...JERK!" Emily said as she shook her finger at someone only she saw standing near the window.

"Guess somebody probably ought to go tell the nurse," Liz said.

Chapter 81

"I have to go now, mother. One day soon you will understand. And you will be recognized for the role you have played in the fulfilling of God's will."

"But don't you see? Things are different now. Together, we can take control of the group and do all of the things we couldn't do when your father was around."

"Mother," Klass said, "I am not coming back. You need to accept the fact that is just not going to happen."

"But, Klassee," Adrianna said, "you don't need to do what you are doing out there. You don't need those people. If you just come..."

"Don't call me Klasee, mother. My name is Klass. And I do not need these people, they need me. God had given me everything I need, mother. He has shown..."

"And this religious talking you do now, you don't need to do that with me. I am your mother, remember. And I know what you are doing with that..."

"You know nothing, mother."

"Klass!"

"You know only the lies that you and father have known your entire lives. Those lies were more important to the two of you than anything else. Including me."

"Klass, no. You were the most important thing in my life. And still are. That's why you need to come home now. Come home, Klass. Before this all goes too far. I am just thinking of what is best for you."

"No. God knows what is best for me. Not you."

He heard her stand up and begin pacing.

"So. This is how much you care about your mother. After all that I did for you. After all of the times I picked you up and cleaned up behind you when you messed up. In school. That job with the Senator. Those women. You are just like your father. Only your father just tried to convince everyone else that he was God's gift to the world. You actually believe it!"

"I am…"

"NO! You are nothing. Not any more. Because of your stupid god-war thing, I may end up losing everything I have worked for, everything I have created. But do you care? No. Are you man enough to come back and help your mother when she needs you the most? No. You are going to…"

"Mother, I need to go…"

"NO! Don't you dare! If you turn your back on me now, I swear I will…"

"I need to go, mother. I will pray for you."

"PRAY FOR ME! You listen to me! You need to come home. NOW! You need…Klass? Klass, do you hear me? KLASS?"

Chapter 82

"Am I dead?" Emily said.

"No, you're not dead," Chambers said.

"Good! When I saw your faces here I knew it couldn't be heaven, so I was kinda worried."

"Yeah," Reyes said, "she's going to be okay."

"Did I hear something about some kind of gun you have that can stop the devices, or did I dream that?"

"You could hear us talking?"

"It was more like I was listening to a movie that kept fading in and out, but yeah, kinda."

"Yes, we think we can stop the devices before they are used," Reyes said. "And we have people ready to move into the place where the trucks come from. But we don't think they may have another place that we haven't located yet. So we're stuck."

"Can you get me something to drink?" Emily said. "I need something."

"Here you go," Liz said as she handed Emily the glass of ice water.

"I was thinking of something a little stronger, maybe?" Emily said.

"There will be time for that later," Chambers said. "Right now we're trying to find out where you've been since this morning."

"Oh, yeah," Emily said. "Where am I now?"

"Back in New Orleans," Liz said.

"Really?" Emily said. "The last thing I remember was...wait...let me think...yeah...I was with Klass."

"You were with VanHollings?" Reyes said. "When? Where?"

"I don't know. It was..."

"Take a minute and think. Do you remember where you were when you were with him?"

"No, that's what I was going to say, I woke up in a house and he was there. We went outside and he showed me the army, then we ate lunch, and then...I'm here."

"Okay," Chambers said. "Let's take this one piece at a time. How did you get to the house?"

"I remember opening the door to the taxi. I was pushed by something, then felt the stick and the next thing I knew I was in the house."

"Okay," Chambers said. "Klass was there, and you went outside. What do you remember about outside?"

"Lots of trees, blue skies with big clouds. I think we were on top of a big hill, but there were so many trees I couldn't really tell. There were lots of people and buildings. But I didn't see most of them."

"What do you mean?" Reyes said. "How do you know you didn't see all of them?"

"Klass told me. I said there must be a thousand people in his army out there. He said five thousand, but they were out in the trees somewhere with the other buildings and stuff. Can I have that water again?"

Liz handed Emily the glass.

"You said something about an army," Chambers said. "That was the people you saw?"

"Yeah, all men. He said the army was men over the age of eighteen, and from the right kind of families, and I can guess what that means."

"Okay," Chambers said. "Did you notice..."

"And he said the rest of the army was at the other camp, but I don't know how many..."

"The other camp?" Reyes said. "So there are more. Did he say how many camps they had?"

"He just said the other camp," Emily said. "So I think just the two."

"And we don't know which one you were at," Chambers said. "Did you have your phone with..."

"Yeah," Emily said. "but he said they disabled it."

"Can't trace that then," Reyes said. "Is there anything else you can tell us that might help determine where you were?"

"Not that I can think of," Emily said. "It was just pretty..."

"Did you have your bracelet on?" Liz said. "I mean, while you were there?"

"My bracelet, yeah, I guess so. Why?"

Liz got up, walked to the window, and opened her laptop on the windowsill.

"We tracked Klass' plane, and it landed in Marion while you were in D. C. and didn't leave there. But we know they have at least one other plane, probably more."

"So," Chambers said, "we know you were at one of their camps. But we don't know if you were at the one we know about in Missouri, or if you were at..."

"She wasn't in Missouri," Liz said from across the room.

"What?" Chambers said. "How do you know that?"

"The plane took her to Marion."

"Okay," Reyes said. "But that still leaves us..."

"Want to know where she was?" Liz said.

"Are you telling me you think you know where?"

"Want to see the coordinates?" Liz said as she held the laptop in front of them.

"How sure are you of this?" Chambers said. "I mean, how accurate is this?"

"Oh, within eight or nine feet, I guess," Liz said. "Five or six if we're lucky."

"How did you get this?" Daryl said. "How did you find it?"

"The bracelet," Liz said.

"My bracelet?" Emily said. "You can track it? How did they miss the signal it was sending out?"

"Because there is no signal," Liz said.

They stared at Liz.

"Ok, look," Liz said. "If anyone looks at it, or scans it or anything, it's just a bracelet. But, it's made out of a little something I came up came up with back in school. I created it so we could keep track of where the principal was, so we didn't get caught as we did our hacking stuff."

"How does it work?"

"It's what it's made of," Liz said. "It's mostly just copper. But I added something a little something that I can pick up using the program I wrote. I gave this one to Emily so I could kind of test it, but with everything going on I completely forgot about it until just now. But yeah, that's where she was."

"Then, that's the base," Reyes said. "The second base."

"We have some work to do," Chambers said. "Graham, you rest up. Reyes, Krebel, let's talk outside. And Liz, why haven't we heard about this bracelet thing before?"

"Because I'm not sure I trust what the people in charge of things will do with it," Liz said.

Chambers smiled.

"Probably a smart move."

They walked toward the door.

"Hey," Emily said, "I've got one more question before you go. I understand how I got to New Orleans, but what I don't understand is why you are all here. I mean, Liz was already here. But what about the rest of you?"

"I came when Lance called and told me they found you. Used your jet, though it still doesn't have that pool."

"And Daryl and I came to see what we might find out about last night, because of, well that's why we're here."

"Last night?" Emily said. "What about last night? Because of what?"

They closed the door as Reyes walked back to Emily.

"We were going to tell you later," Reyes said, "but there were some problems here in town last night. In the Quarter."

"What kind of problems?" Emily said.

"It looks like at least one of the more radical groups got all stirred up by what Klass has been doing, and started their own little war."

"Come on," Emily said. "What do you mean?"

"A bunch of them spent a couple of hours attacking anyone they found around some of the gay places, and some of the other places they believe need to be cleaned out. The party places, the occult places, things like that."

"Why were you waiting to tell me about it?" Emily said.

"Because," Reyes said, "one of the people they found was someone you know. Em, they attacked Angelique."

"Angelique! Is she okay?"

"She's still in pretty rough shape, but they say she's going to pull through. She's down the hall in…"

"I want to see her!" Emily said as she started to stand.

"No," Chambers said. "You need to rest until you…"

"I AM GOING TO SEE HER!" Emily said. "Either help me up or get the hell out of my way!"

Reyes and Chambers looked at each other.

"Get her arm," Chambers said.

Angelique was in the bed with a collection of tubes and wires leading to pieces of equipment. Bandages covered most of her head, but Emily saw the bruises covering most of her face. Angelique's eyes were dark and swollen.

"What happened?" Emily said.

"She was at her store when they got there," Reyes said. "They told her they were going inside and burn it down, but she stood in the doorway and tried to stop them. This is what happened."

"Come on," Chambers said. "You need rest so you can go out and find the people that did this. That's your plan, isn't it?"

They walked from the room and turned to go back to Emily's room. They heard noise behind them and Emily turned. A nurse was talking to someone leaning against the wall.

"You cannot stay here," the nurse said. "I'm sorry but if you aren't family, you have to wait out in the waiting room. I have told you three times now. Do I need to call security?"

Emily stopped.

"What?" Reyes said as Emily pulled away and walked down the hall.

"Graham," Reyes said.

"Aw, just let her go," Chambers said. "It's not worth the fight. Come on, we have a lot of work to do."

"Let me see if I can help," Emily said to the nurse. She smiled at the man.

"Well, hello Captain Bonatemps," Emily said. "You're here to check on Angelique?"

"They hurt her," Antoine Jean Bonatemps DuCheine said.

"Who did? Did you see them?"

"They hurt her real bad. She was standin' there. They yelled. He knocked her down. He kicked her. Kicked her a lot."

"Who did that, Captain? Do you know who they were?"

"The bad one. The bad one was the one that kicked her. His face. I saw his face. A bad man."

"You recognized him? Who was he, Captain? Tell me so I can make him pay for what he did."

The man looked at the floor and tried to to curl up in a ball.

"Captain, can you tell me who..."

"He is bad. I know. If I tell you he will find me and..."

"Captain, look at me. Please, look at me."

He raised his head until his eyes met hers.

"Captain, I promise you that he will not hurt you. No one will hurt you. I promise you. But I need to know who it was so he does not hurt anyone else. Can you tell me who it was? Or tell me something about him?"

"Cop," the man said.

"He was a cop?" Emily said. "You mean, a cop you know?"

"A cop. I see him every day. A bad cop."

"Do you know his name?"

"No," he said as his eyes fell.

"Captain, please, try and remember. Do you remember anything else about him, about what happened to Angelique?"

"They called him man…when they ran away."

"Man?"

"Man…mans…maynas…something like that is what they called him."

"Maynas?" Emily said.

The neuron fired somewhere deep inside her brain. She felt it more than thought it.

"Manzaneres? Is that what they called him? Did they call him Manzanares?

The man's face lowered again as he nodded.

"Bad man. He kicked her."

Emily wasn't sure if it was Manzanares or the effects from the drug, but she knew she needed to sit down. The Captain left after Emily promised she would stay to protect Angelique. She walked into Angelique's room, pulled a chair next to the bed, sat down, and closed her eyes.

She could see the waves crashing on the beach. The wind was…

"Graham! Wake up!" the voice said. "Come on, wake up! "

Emily opened her eyes and saw Chambers.

"What? I just sat down. I just…"

"Its just before three, Graham. You've been asleep for four about hours. And now its time to wake up. We are making our move. Come on."

"Our move? What move?"

"I'll bring up to to speed on the way. We need to get moving!"

Chapter 83

The semi was on I-40 just West of Russellville, headed toward the warehouse in Conway. They would unload there and the van would continue on to Little Rock. They were watching the moonlight shining on the surface of Lake Dardanelle, and did not notice the small, panel truck slowly pulling past them.

"Those people really tick me off," the driver said.

"Who's that?"

"Like the idiot in that truck there. They do it all the time. They start coming around you and then they get about half-way around, slow down, and just hang there. I just ticks me off. Either pass me or stay behind me!"

"One of these days they're gonna cause a wreck," the passenger said.

"That's what I mean. They pop a tire, or we pop one. Anything like that could happen and, bang, we're over there in the lake or something."

"COME ON STUPID!" the driver said. "GET IN GEAR!"

The three men in the truck did not hear him shout. The driver kept his eye on holding the truck in position. The second man stood near the hatch cut between the cab of the truck and the back where he could talk with both the driver, and the third man who stood in the back of the truck, holding one of the weapons Daryl had gotten from his friend.

"Finally!" the semi driver said.

The man with the weapon held it steady as the panel truck slowly pass the length of the semi. There was no sound, other than a slight hum none of the others could hear. The driver glanced toward the hatchway as he pulled away from the semi.

"Did we get it?" he said.

"We covered the whole length of the trailer, so if it was in there, yeah, we got it."

"There's no way to know for sure, though, right?" the driver said.

"Not without stopping them and looking around inside, and I'm thinking that's not on our list of options."

"Okay," the driver said. "Go ahead and let 'em know."

The man by the hatchway pulled out his phone.

"Santa," he said, "this is Rudolph. The lightning has struck."

Chapter 84

"I have to say, Colonel," Emily said, "I am impressed that you were able to get that much done so quickly."

"Well," Chambers said, "we pretty much had everyone in position to move, we just had to wait until we had the location of that other camp. When Liz gave us that, we just put the pieces in motion. Reyes gets the credit for a lot of it, along with his buddy Krebel. Daryl getting us those weapons gave us the idea for just how to do what we're doing. As long as they work."

"What do you mean? I thought they did work."

"Oh, yeah, the weapons do what they're supposed to. But we don't have any way to make sure they actually knocked the device out when we try to zap it."

"When are they going to do that?"

"Already been done," Chambers said. "We started tracking the truck when it left the camp, and one of our teams hit it about twenty minutes ago."

"If it did work," Emily said, "I mean if they did knock it out, the people in the van aren't going to notice that it's dead?"

"Graham, there comes a point where you just have to do everything you can possibly do, and then just cross your fingers."

"Yeah, I'm familiar with that strategy."

Chambers heard his phone and picked it up.

"Chambers."

"Ok," he said. "Yeah, Graham and I are on the plane now. Should be at the target in thirty minutes. Graham? Well, she's the only one of us who has actually met this Klass face-to-face, so, yeah, just to make sure. Yeah, its still Little Rock as far as we know, that's what their flight plan says. I don't know, but those have been accurate so far. You're in position? Good. As they get closer we'll try to keep you near enough to move in nice and fast-like. Yeah, you too."

"So," Emily said, "Reyes and Daryl are with the group following the device, and their job is to make sure the device doesn't fire?"

"Right," Chambers said, "and to pick up the people from the truck."

"Do we have any idea just where they are headed to?", Emily said. "Other than Little Rock, I mean?"

"No. That's why we're going to keep several eyes on that van so we can try to keep Reyes' team close enough to get to them in time once they do stop."

"You have any hunches?"

"Well, I know where I'd go if it was me, but I would really like to be wrong this time."

"Your thinking the base, right?" Emily said.

Chambers smiled.

"Like I said, it's what I'd do. I can't think of a better way to make one more big point than by taking out an Air Force Base. Especially since it is a central training base and the home of the Nineteenth Airlift Wing, the largest C-130 transport outfit in the world. Can you think of anything better?"

"Nope," Emily said. "That's the first thing that came in mind when you said they were headed to Little Rock. If this was just another attack, maybe not. But he said this was the last one before they moved to the next phase, so yeah, my money's on the base."

"You're clear on our part of this too, right?" Chambers said.

"Yeah, we're landing at..."

Chamber reached for his phone.

"Chambers."

"They did? Yeah, that's what we want to do. Okay. Well, it could be a last minute diversion, something to throw us off the trail. But I really don't think they know we're anywhere around, so we'll go with it. Right."

"Something happen?" Emily said.

"They just changed their flight plan," Chambers said. "Now they're landing at Adams Field instead of Little Rock Municipal. It's still Little Rock, just eight or so miles further South. Must have been some kind of problem."

"Or," Emily said, "it's further away from the base, right?"

"Yeah," Chambers said," about eight...oh...I think I see what you're getting at."

"Yeah, if this is their last attack, and they're using the base to make a big noise, they probably want to make it as big as they can."

"So," Chambers said, "they decided they wanted to be further away from it when it goes. I go with that. It just changes where we land. Everything else goes forward as planned. We will land at Adams before Klass' plane gets there, and the second plane will join us as soon as we have solid confirmation Klass is there. We should be able to take them with our team, but the second will reinforce if we need them. They'll also handle any collateral that might need dealing with."

"So, one more time," Chambers said. "We get in the cars waiting for us, and as quickly as we can we get to where their plane ends up parking. Your job is to ID Klass. As soon as we do that, we give the signal to the other teams to move in. Reyes' team makes sure the device is taken care of, and the other teams hit the two camps in Missouri and Illinois. It has to be done at the same time, and we cannot do anything, or even let them know we are around, until you tell me your absolutely positive Klass is with that plane. Clear?"

"Just one thing, I guess," Emily said.

"What's that?"

"I don't have a weapon. We left in…"

"You'll have one when we land," Chambers said, "But, that's the one other thing that makes this thing interesting. We are not going to be able to use traditional arms to take them down. We're at a public airport, and there will be so many civilians within range, we can't risk any shots missing a target. We'll use shorter range, non-lethals. Besides, we want these people alive."

"What if they aren't worried about stray shots?" Emily said.

"Then they don't have the same views on protecting innocent people that we do," Chambers said. "And, they don't have to answer to the same people we do."

Chambers looked out the window.

"Won't be much longer. I need to talk to the team."

Chapter 85

"How you feeling this morning, Grandpa? What did the doctor say?"

"He said I had to give up the whiskey. He didn't say anything about the sex this time."

"Seriously, what did he say?"

"Oh, the usual. Something about my rhythm being out again or something. He wants me to go back this morning for another test. I figure if it was serious he would have done it yesterday, so..."

"What time this morning? You are going for that test, aren't you? Do you need me to..."

"Ronnie," Grandpa put down his coffee. "I want to tell you something, and I want you to listen to me. I appreciate you worrying about me like you do. And, honestly, it means a hell of a lot to me."

"I just..."

"But," Grandpa said, "and this is the part I want you to understand, I am not afraid of dying. You know, I've lived longer than both my parents, my brothers and sisters, and your grandmother. And, Ronnie, I'll tell you something about your grandmother I would absolutely deny if she was here. You know, she could be a cantankerous old woman when she put her mind to it. Her whole side of the family was that way. They believed they knew more than anyone else around them, and there was nothing they loved more in the world than a good argument. Your mother has some of that in her. But Ronnie, as many times I can remember sitting at my workbench in the basement just to get away from her arguing, I miss her. When she died eleven years ago next month, it just, well, I just miss her."

"I'm sorry Grandpa."

"I don't know if all that talking they do about getting back together in heaven is true or not, but it's nice to think about talking to her again. But, what I want you to know is that I'm not afraid of all this. My heart, and all. Yes, I'll do the tests and do what they tell me to do, well, most of it. But not because I'm afraid. Do you understand?"

"Yes, grandpa, I understand. I'll still pester you about your heart, but I understand."

"Okay, then. We have things to catch up on. I'm afraid it looks like poor Adrianna VanHollings is starting to fall apart."

"Yeah," Ronnie said, "but the others in the group have started getting things under control. And like you said yesterday, that's a good thing."

"Yes," Grandpa said, "just a few anonymous messages to a couple of them seem to have gotten their attention."

"I wondered if we had anything to do with it."

"We do what we can do, Ronnie. What's going on with the plans to stop Klass?"

"Well, we helped get those secret guns into the right hands, and it looks like things are moving forward. And, I hadn't realized that Liz, that young programmer, was one of the people the group has been monitoring and preparing as an influencer. I can see why. It helps me feel a little better about the whole thing. I mean, if the group hadn't helped get her to this place..."

"That's right," Grandpa said. "We could not do what we do without them. I'm glad you are beginning to understand."

"Me too. But, you know the one thing I do not understand is Klass, and why he took Graham to their camp. I mean, I know he has his issues, but why would he take that kind of risk? And then let her go? What is he thinking?"

"We've talked about it before. He's not thinking, not really. In those groups, people aren't afraid of being accused of not thinking. They are afraid of being accused of not believing. To them, disbelief is the sign of the enemy. And if you risk thinking about what you are doing, you risk questioning it. And that might lead to no longer believing. So he didn't think about risk. He wanted to show off, to win another convert to the cause. And he let her go because he truly believed she was going to come back to him."

"Well," Ronnie said, "the way things are going this morning, she is going to. But not quite the way he expected."

"Yes," Grandpa said. "You need to go keep an eye on that, and I have a test to take. Give the kids a hug for me?"

"I always do."

Chapter 86

"Target has turned North on four-four-zero, Northbound," the voice on the radio said.

"Well, Graham, I was beginning to doubt our thinking when they headed straight downtown, but it's beginning to look like we had it right after all. They just turned back towards the base."

Emily sat in the SUV with Chambers and three other team members, parked in a lot at the corner of the group of hangars on the North side of the airport. Reyes, Daryl, and their team was traveling two miles behind the van, staying out of sight but close enough to move in when it was time. They all listened to the radio updates of the van's movements from the controller of the drone following high above.

"Target turning Northbound on highway six-seven."

Chambers felt his phone.

"Chambers."

"Bill, it's Lance. We need to talk."

"What's wrong? Is there a problem?"

"Not exactly, but we want to change the plan."

"Change it? Now? Why? Wait, let me put this on speaker so Graham and the rest of the team can hear."

Chambers pressed the button.

"Okay, go."

"Its Daryl, and that stomach of his. Something has been eating at him for a while, and I'm beginning to agree with it."

"What do you want to change?"

"We are convinced they are heading for the air force base. We're not sure how they plan to get through the security, but we'll bet our pensions that's where they are going. And once they get inside, it's going to be tough for us to stay with them and keep out of site. So, we want to stop shadowing and move our team to the base now, so we..."

"Do it."

"What, that easy?" Reyes said.

"Graham and I came to that conclusion over an hour ago. And Reyes, I suggest you locate somewhere in the area of the tower. It's a likely target, but it will put you where you can easily relocate if you have to."

"The tower it is. Anything on your end yet?"

"We're in place," Chambers said. "Last I heard they should be on the ground anytime now."

"Let us know when you confirm Klass is there," Reyes said.

"I'll call you right after I call my wife and tell her."

Chambers put away the phone and listened to the reports from the drone.

Fifteen miles to the North, the van exited Highway Sixty-Seven onto Vandenburg Boulevard.

"They're heading toward the gate," Chambers said. "They shouldn't get through."

"Target is at the front gate," The radio said. "Passing through."

"They have help," Chambers said. "That's the only way they would get through that quickly. They have someone inside."

Chambers grabbed the radio.

"Team One, did you hear? They just came through the main gate. That means they have one or more people inside the base. Stay sharp."

"Roger," Lance Reyes said.

Chambers put down the phone. "I'm going to find out who..."

There's the plane!" Emily said.

"Okay everyone," Chambers said, "it's show time."

Chambers grabbed the radio.

"All teams, this is Team Lead. Both eggs are in the nest. Hold for confirmation."

The jet rolled down the runway and turned onto the taxiway leading to the group of hangars.

"Yeah, that's the plane," Emily said as it taxied past the lot.

"But is Klass on it?" Chambers said.

"Team Lead, this is Team One. The target is at the tower. The target is at the tower."

"Shit!" Chambers said. "We can't move until we know if he is here."

Emily watched the plane through binoculars as it turned from the taxiway and slowly pulled into the parking area twelve hundred feet away.

Emily lowered the binoculars and turned to Chambers.

"Colonel, I was wondering. Don't you and your teams usually practice things like this before you actually do them?"

"Twenty or thirty times," Chambers said. "Why?"

"Just curious," Emily said as she lifted the binoculars.

The plane turned and slowly came to a stop.

"Graham?" Chambers said.

The doorway opened.

"Graham?" Chambers said.

The stairway slowly lowered into place.

"Graham?" Chambers said.

And Klass VanHollings stepped onto the ground.

"He's here!" Emily said. "VanHollings is here."

"You are certain?" Chambers said. "We don't want to…"

He stopped when he saw the look on her face.

"All teams, this is Team Lead. We have confirmation. Repeat, we have confirmation. All teams move in thirty."

Chambers put down the radio, glanced at Emily, then at the three men in the back seat.

"Let's do this!" Chambers said.

Chapter 87

"Who is there?" Angelique asked as she tried to see the face of the person sitting next to her bed. "Who are you?"

"It's Liz, Angelique, remember me?"

Angelique closed her eyes and took a deep breath. Her face twisted from the pain of the small movement.

"Yes, I remember."

"I'm glad you are awake," Liz said. "Emily will be relieved to hear it, too. I need to go tell the nurse that you..."

"I dreamed of her," Angelique said. "Just now. Of Emily. Is she okay?"

"She is with the others. They are going to stop what is happening. And then they will find the people who did this to you. Do you want anything? A drink?"

Angelique slowly moved her head from side to side, the pain again showing on her face.

"Those people. They came to my shop. They are so angry. So very angry."

Liz moved closer to hear the soft voice.

"But they do not understand. They do not understand where their anger comes from. Who is making them carry that anger."

Angelique raised an arm to wipe her mouth and held her hand still as she looked at the tubes and wires.

"So very sad. These people. They do not understand."

She took another slow breath.

"They attack those who choose to not be angry. Those who chose to love. The voices tell them to believe. Believe things that only make them more angry. I pray other voices will speak to them. Voices without anger. They do not understand. So very sad."

Angelique slept.

Chapter 88

They stood by the plane, joined hands, and prayed.

Klass turned North to face the Little Rock Air Force Base, and raised his hands in the air over his head.

He lowered them and looked at the group.

"Remember this day, my friends. This is the day God allowed me to lead you into his new nation. Today, all of our work bears holy fruit."

He raised his hands in the air as tears rolled down his face.

The car carrying the two men pulled from the parking lot across the street from the tower. A black SUV appeared in front of them and a second stopped behind them. They said nothing as they were pulled from the car.

The helicopters were the first thing they heard. As they looked up to locate their location, the men in full battle gear appeared from the trees around the camp. The holy army that had been trained at the camp had not been trained for this kind of battle. It ended before the last helicopter reached the ground.

As they had practiced, most of them ran into the cavern when they heard the first helicopter approach. They closed the massive doors and prepared to defend themselves from the godless attackers. The steel and concrete doors were strong. The men inside the caverns fought from the fortress they had built, firing their weapons from the small holes and tunnels they had created in the hillside from inside the cave. A man with a loudspeaker ordered them to surrender. They did not surrender. The helicopter came low over the trees and released the weapon. The massive, steel and concrete doors disappeared. The fighting was over.

"WHAT DO YOU MEAN IT DID NOT WORK?" Klass said to the man who had approached him.

"They just said..."

"NO! THIS CANNOT BE. GOD WILL NOT ALLOW THIS TO..."

He saw people moving toward them from across the lot. He recognized one of those people.

"NOOOO!" Klass said as he ran up the stairway into his plane.

The other men with Klass began to run. They ran directly into the second team coming around the hangar from the other direction. A gun was pulled but no shots were fired.

The engines spooled up on the jet and it began to slowly move toward the taxiway as the teams fired at it with their short-range, non-lethal weapons.

"He's getting away!" Emily said. "Shoot it! Get a gun!"

"We can't do that," Chambers said. "Too much risk if..."

"So, you're just going to let him get away?"

"Dammit, Graham," Chambers said. "I don't like it any more than you do. We should have moved in sooner."

Emily grabbed her phone.

"Did you get him?" Reyes said.

"NO! He made it to his plane, he's getting away. Can you do something?"

"From here? Graham, I'm fifteen miles away. Wait, Daryl has something..."

"I don't want to..."

"Emily?" Daryl said, "Are you still with Chambers?"

"Yeah, why?"

"And his car?"

"His car? Yeah, it's not far."

"Emily, now listen carefully. There is another gun in the back of Chambers' car. One of the zap guns."

"In the car?"

"Go get it."

"But I..."

"Go get it now! I'll wait. Tell me when you have it."

Emily ran.

"Where is she going?" Chambers said to the team member standing next to him.

"Okay, Okay, I'm at the car. I see the gun."

"Now listen, you're only going to get one shot at this."

"Okay. You mean...?

"Pick up the gun. You got it?"

"Yeah."

"Do you see the blue button, on the side, the right side, close to the trigger."

"Yeah, I see it."

"Push it."

"Okay, I pushed it."

"Okay, you just armed the weapon."

"I did what? You mean…"

"Just keep your fingers away from the trigger until you're ready to fire it, do you understand?"

"Fingers, yeah."

"Now, the dial on up in front of that button. The round dial with the numbers on it. Do you…"

"Yeah, I got it."

"Turn it clockwise as far as it will go."

"Okay. Clockwise, right?"

"Yes, clockwise. Did you turn it?"

"Yes, as far as it will go. What does that do?"

"That sets the farthest range. I'm not sure just how far away the plane is going to be when it takes off."

"When it…you mean you want me to shoot the thing down?"

"It's the only way to stop him, Emily. And if he gets away, well, we just can't let that happen, and you're the one we apparently all elected to do it. Now, one more thing. Do you see the targeting reticle, the…"

"The what?"

"The thing that looks like a little ladder, up on top about half way down. It's got…"

"Got it. Lift it up?"

"Yeah, up. Now, this is important. When you aim at the plane, center it in the space between the top two rungs on that ladder. The one highest up. That should account for the distance."

"Yeah, okay. What next?"

"Okay, can you see the plane?"

"Just a sec. Yeah. It's just starting down the runway, about to lift-off."

"Okay then. Zap it!"

"NOW? You think…"

"Just do it, Emily! We'll argue about it later over coffee somewhere. Put it in the top box and pull the damn trigger."

Emily took a breath and raised the gun. She watched through the small space on the site as the jet's wheels left the runway. She watched as the wheels began to fold-up into the body of the plane. She closed her eyes, took a deep breath, then opened them.

She pulled the trigger.

Nothing happened other than a slight vibration and a low humming sound that lasted less than a second. She looked at the gun and wondered what she had done wrong.

She looked back up just as the plane disappeared behind another hangar. Then she saw the billows of dark smoke begin to curl into the sky.

Chapter 89

"I have to go!"

"What's wrong Ronnie? Has something happened? What was that phone call?"

"The hospital. It's grandpa. I need to go."

"It's late. It's after eleven. I can call Sue to come and stay with the…"

"Don't have time. I'll call you when I find out what's going on."

The hallways were quiet when he got off the elevator. He walked toward the nurse's station.

"You wouldn't be Ronnie by any chance?" the nurse said.

"I thought you might be. He's over there in two twelve. He's been asking about you."

Ronnie walked to the door and stepped inside. His grandfather was lying in the bed. His eyes were closed. Ronnie let out his breath when he saw the blankets slowly rise and fall.

"Grandpa?" he said as he moved to the bed.

The older man spoke, but his words were muffled by the mask pumping pure oxygen. Grandpa slid the mask up until it rested against his forehead.

"Are you sure you should…"

"Ronnie, they shouldn't have called you this late. But I'm glad they did."

"What happened?"

"Oh, your grandmother must have heard me talking about her this morning. She probably made enough noise to pull some strings, and…"

Grandpa closed his eyes and took in a deep breath, then slowly eased it out.

"She always was a hard woman to say no too."

"Has the doctor been here yet?"

"Ronnie, I have something I want to give you. Its there on the table next to the glass of water."

Ronnie turned.

"The chain? The gold necklace chain with the coin on it? I guess it's a coin."

"Yes. Bring it here."

Ronnie handed the chain to his grandfather. Grandpa held it up in his hands.

"I want you to have this, Ronnie. I want you to take it, and wear it."

"Grandpa I don't..."

"Do it for me, will you? Here, let me see you put it on."

Ronnie took the chain in his hands and looked at it.

"Please, put it on."

He opened the small clasp, held the chain up around his neck and refastened the clasp.

"Good. That is good."

The old man closed his eyes and took another deep breath.

"Ronnie," he said as he opened his eyes. "Promise me you will wear it always. I can't tell you why. But please promise me."

"I will Grandpa. But, hey, you shouldn't be giving things away yet. I'm sure..."

"Ronnie. You have made me a very proud man. Thank you."

Ronnie looked at the floor and blinked away what he was feeling. He looked back up as his grandfather closed his eyes, took in a deep breath, and eased it out.

Ronnie hesitated, looking at his grandfather. Then he pushed the button.

A nurse walked in, looked at the man in the bed, and held his wrist in her hand. She looked at Ronnie and shook her head.

Chapter 90

"YOU KILLED MY SON!"

Emily held the phone away from her ear.

"Mrs. VanHollings, we had no other…"

"NO! YOU MURDERED HIM! YOU…"

"That is not…"

"The wonderful Emily Graham," Adrianna said. "You promised me you would help me and save my son, and instead you are the one who killed him. You! Emily Graham. You lied to me!"

"I never said…"

"I should have let them kill you when they wanted to. Then you would be the one gone and not my son."

"Who wanted to…"

"Oh no, Emily Graham. You get nothing more from me. Nothing except the same thing you gave to my son. You took my son, and now I will make you pay. You have no idea what I can do, Emily Graham! You have no idea of what I can do, and how much I control! But you are going to learn…you are going to see what I will do to the woman who killed my son!

Silence.

"GOOD!" Adrianna said. "You have nothing to say. Very soon you will have nothing to say to anyone, Emily Graham. And it will be the same for your friends, those who helped you murder my son. You have no idea what I am going to do to you, Emily Graham. I have power. You have no idea what I can do!"

Adrianna threw the phone on the floor.

"RAUL!" she said.

The door opened and Raul Weith walked in.

"Something you need, Mrs. VanHollings."

"I want you to kill her, the woman who killed my son. That Emily Graham. I want you to go get her, bring her here to me, so I can watch her die, just like she watched my son die. Go get her Raul. Do that for me. Go get her. Bring her here. Bring her so I can watch her. Bring her to me."

Weith moved to Adrianna VanHollings and held her arm in his hand.

"Mrs. VanHollings. You know I will do whatever you ask me to do. I always have. But it is late tonight. And you have had a very difficult day. I will bring Emily Graham to you, but tomorrow. Tonight, why don't you rest a moment on the sofa and let me get you a drink. Something to take away the pain."

Adrianna looked at Weith.

"Yes, yes, that is probably best. We will let Emily Graham lie awake all night wondering how much longer she will be alive. Yes, Raul, you always know the best. Thank you."

Adrianna sat on the sofa. Weith walked back with two glasses.

"You don't mind if I join you, do you?" he said.

"No, I don't mind."

"Good. Now drink. And we will talk about happier things."

Adrianna VanHollings lifted her glass toward Weith, and drank. She smiled.

"Ah, you know my favorite, don't you?"

"Yes, I know," Weith said as he sat in the chair next to the sofa.

Adrianna drank again, and smiled at Weith.

"You know, its been always...oops...I mean it's alway was the...oh my, I don't whats come over..."

Adrianna looked at her glass. She looked again at Weith, as he stood from his chair.

"You," she said. "You did..."

Adrianna's tried to focus her eyes as Weith put his glass on the table.

"Why?" Adrianna said. "Why?"

Weith smiled as he took the glass from her hand.

"There were just too many mistakes. Too many mistakes."

Chapter 91

Dasilva was waiting at the fence when Emily walked from the plane.

"Did you get what you need?" she said.

"Enough," Dasilva said. "We've just been waiting for you to get here. I knew you wanted to be in on it."

Reyes and the teams were still in Little Rock, finishing things up at the airport and the base. Daryl was getting the non-existent zap-guns back to his friends. Chambers was coordinating with the people doing the work at the two camps. After a brief discussion with Chambers, he agreed to let Emily fly back to New Orleans, and meet with the group later to fully debrief.

"Yeah," Emily said as they walked to the car, "did you have any problems with city?"

"None," Dasilva said. "No matter what some of them may actually believe, they didn't have any choice but cooperate after we presented what we had. In fact, they've gotten downright righteous about it. Top brass said they were horrified to find this kind of behavior in the force, and would do whatever we said to set an example."

"Mighty big of them," Emily said.

"Yeah, they're being very nice. I think some of them are worried about what we're going to find as we keep investigating."

"How are you wanting to do this?" Emily said. "Do you mind if I go in first?"

"That's the plan. I figured you would like that."

"Yeah, thanks," Emily said.

"We'll be close behind, just in case."

"Okay. I don't think it will be a problem, but I also didn't think I would be doing this. So, yeah, thanks."

The cars went down Esplanade Avenue, turned onto Dauphine, and stopped just before reaching St. Ann.

"They say he's on the corner down there on Bourbon," Dasilva said, "helping with the investigation of the attacks."

Emily looked at Dasilva.

"That's where Angelique's store is."

"Yeah," Dasilva said. "The guy's got balls."

"And I'm about to kick'em."

Emily got out, and slowly walked along St. Ann. She stopped at the corner where the yellow tape stretched across the road. She looked through the doors of the corner cafe where they had met for lunch the day they had first came to town. She turned around and looked at the shattered windows of the shop across the street, and the door with dark bloodstains on the stoop.

He was standing just around the corner, in front of the store. He was writing something in a notebook as he talked with someone in white coveralls.

Emily lifted the yellow tape and walked toward the corner.

"Hey, Manzanares, what's up?"

"Emily!" he said. "I heard you were out somewhere chasing bad guys."

"Yeah, keeps a girl busy, you know? So, what you got?"

"Oh, that voodoo woman here got herself in trouble the other night. Some folks were acting up, you know what happens on Bourbon Street. Well, apparently she decided to quiet them down or something, and they didn't like it."

"She started it?"

"Looks that way. I mean, it sounds like the group was going to far at times, but she should have just called us instead of taking things into her own hands. People never learn, do they?"

"Yeah, some don't. Any idea who the guys were?"

"Just a bunch of out-of-towners who had a little too much of Bourbon Street and let it get out of control. You know how that goes."

"Yeah. Have they figure out which one of them kicked her around?"

"No, but one of them is bound to let..."

Emily looked at Manzanares.

"Which one kicked her? Hell, it was probably most of them. But, we'll find..."

"Well, I don't know. The person who saw it told me it was just the one guy. Just the one."

"Yeah? Well, we've talked with a dozen who say they saw the attack, and they all have different stories. You know that anytime..."

"Attack? I thought you said she started it?"

216

"Yeah, well, I meant what happened after she provoked them. That attack."

Emily looked at him.

"Hey," Manzanares said, "I really need to get back to things here. Why don't we meet for...what? What are you looking at?"

"I'm looking at a no-good, son-of-a-bitch, crooked cop. That's what I'm looking at."

"I don't know what..."

"You kicked her, Manzanares. And you're lying about her provoking anything."

"Now you just wait..."

"You and your buddies were out to show some gays and other weirdos what you thought about them, isn't that what happened?"

"Look, you can't..."

"And when Angelique stood in her doorway, you had to teach her a lesson, didn't you?"

"You don't have anything to..."

"All this time I thought you were one of the good ones. A friend. And now I find out that your just another piece of the same crap I spend every other day having to try and clean-up."

Manzanares stared at Emily.

"Piece of crap? You don't have any idea what you're dealing with, Graham. You don't know who we are, what we are going to do. You need to be care..."

"I know more than you think, Manzanares. I know that the big war you thought you were helping start down here, just got blown all to hell this afternoon."

"What..."

"I know that what you thought was going to happen, isn't going to happen."

"You don't..."

"And Manzanares, I also know what is going to happen to you and those big-assed boots you were wearing when you attacked that innocent woman. You're done, Manzanares."

His face was red. His fists clenched. He leaned toward Emily, then lunged to the left and began running down Bourbon Street. He pushed away the tape and the tourists as he ran. He slowed down when he saw the car at the next corner and the men walking toward him. He turned to climb the metal fence to get to the alley, then saw the men there. He looked back and saw Emily slowly walking toward him with another group. He put his hand on the gun on his belt.

"You can't prove anything, Graham," he said as Emily put the handcuffs on him that Dasliva had handed her. "It's some drunk's word against a cop's. You can't prove anything."

"Officer Manzanares, allow me to introduce myself. I am Special Agent Arturo Dasilva. I have two bits of information you may be interested in. The second one is the information about your rights, which I'll read to you in a minute. But the first piece I have to tell you is that Graham, here, doesn't have to prove a thing. You're problems have nothing to do with Graham. Your problems are things like the video that was taken during your little adventure here. Video of the attack, as well as from the past three years of meetings and conversations you've been involved in. You see, two of your buddies were actually my agents. That, former officer Manzanares, that is your problem. Now, listen carefully as I read you your rights."

Dasilva looks at the little card in his hand.

"Unless you'd like to do this," Dasilva said as he looked at Emily.

"No, but thanks. I have something I need to do."

Angelique did not smile.

"I thought you would be relieved to know we had him?" Emily said.

"Oh, I knew you would catch him," Angelique said.

"Your cards?"

"No, because I know you. But, like I told Liz earlier, it's just so sad. Such a waste. What they are doing that to men like him."

Emily leaned back in the chair.

"You look tired," Angelique said. "Why don't you rest a minute?"

"Me? No, I'm fine. I mean, the past couple of days have been long, but I'm fine. I might just close my eyes for a few minutes though, if you don't mind."

"Do that."

Emily closed her eyes and shrugged her shoulders a couple of times to ease the tightness.

The wind was warm. Her mother and father were standing at the Tiki bar under the palm tree, arguing about the piece of fruit the bartender had put in their drinks. Angelique sat in a beach chair, in the shade of the tree that Ramon Manzanares was handcuffed to. A crowd of people stood nearby, watching Chambers, Reyes, and Daryl dive into the surf to pull sharks out of the water. Daryl called for Emily to help, but she was busy. She was trying to watch Jimmy Buffet sing Brown

Eyed Girl on the stage, while using the huge ray-gun in her arms to shoot down that airplane flying over her head.

Chapter 92

Emily poured the milk on her cereal, refilled her coffee, and sat at her kitchen table. She picked up the remote and turned on the television. The usual morning shows were on, with their usual guest interviews. Emily groaned.

"How can people watch this stuff?" she said out loud.

She flipped through the channels until she saw him. She held the volume button until she could hear what they were saying. He was being interviewed in his official role as a Senator, answering questions about the things that had happened two weeks ago. She put another spoonful of cereal in her mouth.

"It has been a very difficult time," Senator Arthur Murena said, "both professionally and personally."

"Yes, you were familiar with the VanHollings family, weren't you?"

"Yes. I have known the VanHollings for many years. They have been very supportive and helpful, for many of us in leadership. On both sides of the aisle."

"How is that?"

"Both of the VanHollings were, of course, very wealthy. But they both believed that their wealth was just another way they could help improve the welfare of others. They supported many very important programs, and helped those of us in Washington bring about the changes needed to make those improvements."

Emily stopped chewing.

"And you knew their son."

"Yes. A few years ago I helped him with one of the projects the family was trying to develop. It was his first major role. It was an honor to have the opportunity to mentor him."

"There have been rumors that he was someone involved in the things that happened two weeks ago. The attacks that took place in..."

"There are always rumors, Susan. But knowing the VanHollings family as I do, I am certain none of them would have had anything to do with something of that nature. It simply is not in their blood."

Emily swallowed and put down her spoon as he kept talking.

"And we have all seen the early reports from the investigations. We have already found solid evidence linking the attacks to radical elements from outside of this country. We don't yet know if it was someone like North Korea, China, or even someone like Iran, but I can assure you, we will not end the investigation until we know exactly who it was."

"CHINA?" Emily said. "IRAN"?"

"But," the interviewer said, "some wonder about the timing. The fact that…"

"I know where you are going, so let me respond to your question directly. It has been difficult to imagine what happened to the VanHollings family, as quickly as it happened. To see, not one, but all three members of a family taken from us in such a short time is difficult to comprehend. First, Berend VanHollings' heart attack, then the tragic plane crash that took the life of their son. That kind of loss would be profoundly difficult for anyone to endure. Adrianna VanHollings loved her family, and losing them both that quickly, well, it was just too much."

"Too much?" Emily said as got the dishrag from the sink and wiped up the coffee she spilled on the table. "I'll tell you what's too much!"

"I have just one more question, Senator. And it is one that I know every American is asking this morning. After all that has happened, what impact do you believe it is going to have on our country, long term?"

"Impact? Well, I can tell you what impact it has had on me. Perhaps that will help. I can tell you that this has caused me to think even harder about what is truly important to me, both as a Senator, and as a citizen of the United States of America. It has reminded me of what this country is all about. It is a country made of people that no outsider is going to frighten, no matter what kind of foolish things they might try to do. It is a country that, when someone does try something like this, we will spare no effort or expense in hunting them down and seeing they pay the price for what they have done."

Emily stood by the sink.

"Susan, I'll tell you the impact this has had on me. And I will tell every person watching or listening. After what happened, I have rededicated myself to do everything in my power as a United States Senator to end the feelings of division that exist in this country today.

221

Division caused by those who do not believe in what this country stands for. I will spend whatever time I have left, helping to, once again, turn this country into what the founding fathers had in mind when they wrote those words. One nation. Under God."

"Thank you Senator. We have been talking with Senator Arthur Murena about..."

Emily pressed the button and tossed the remote on the couch. She missed.

"Sure!" she said.

She put on her shoes. She brushed her teeth.

"You've got to be freaking kidding me!" she said as she put her phone in her pocket and walked out her front door.

Chapter 93

Ronnie sat at the table.

Each time he heard the door open he turned around. He knew it was not his grandfather, but he turned to look just the same. He looked out the window as he thought about the things his grandfather had said yesterday. Ronnie smiled as he picked up his cup.

"Well grandpa, wherever you and grandma are now, I just hope there's a basement."

He leaned forward to get a napkin and felt the chain against his neck. He pulled it out from his shirt and looked at the little gold coin hanging on the necklace.

"Excuse me," the voice said, "may I join you for a moment?"

The man was older than Ronnie, and had a smile on his face.

"Well, this isn't a good morning to..."

"No, please," the man said, "I understand. I just noticed your necklace there, and wanted to..."

"Oh, this?" Ronnie said. "It belonged to my grandfather. He gave it to me last night. Before he..."

"I'm sorry," the man said. "May I sit down for just a moment? I'd like to show you something."

Ronnie glanced out the window, then at the door that had opened.

"Okay, sure. I'm sorry. You want to show me something? Are you selling..."

Ronnie stopped when the man reached into his shirt and pulled out the chain. It was gold. There was a small, gold coin hanging from it.

"That looks like..."

"May I see yours a second?" the man said. "Just to see?"

Ronnie held the chain in front of him and they compared the two coins.

"They are alike," Ronnie said, "They're the same."

"I thought so," the man said. "They came from the same place."

"The same...the same store? How do you know that?"

"They came from the same man, your grandfather gave this one to me, too."

Ronnie looked at the man.

"He gave it to me when he trained me. I was the first of the two."

"Wait," Ronnie said. "My grandfather gave it to you? The first of two what?"

"With everything we do, one of the most important things is to make sure someone continues our work after we stop. We are to select two people that we will train do just that. Your grandfather gave me this almost twenty years ago. And, you are the second."

"You know about...I mean..."

"Yes, and I know about you. Your grandfather never stopped talking about you. It is really nice to finally meet you in person."

Ronnie looked at the necklaces.

"I was so sorry to hear about last night," the man said. "Oh, my name is Nessas. Nessas Kharondas."

"That sounds Greek," Ronnie said.

"Yes, it is. I met your grandfather just after my family came to this country. Along with training me, he was a great help to us as we learned how to get started here. He was a good man."

"Yes, he was. My name is Ron...oh, you already know that don't you? Sorry."

Nessas Kharondas smiled.

"Don't worry about it, this is a lot to take in. I would like to talk more, but I will wait until you have..."

"No, it's okay. Please, stay a while. Really. It's kind of nice to talk about him like this. No one else..."

"I understand. Thanks. Let me go get a drink."

Nessas ordered a drink from the barista, and walk back to the table. Nessas looked at the sticker on the side of the cup as he sat down.

"Did you get this message this morning? About the..."

"The one about Atlanta? Yeah. You too?"

"Just did," Nessas said. "I wonder what we can do about it?"

"I was thinking about that before you came in."

Ronnie drank from his coffee.

"You know, when things like this came up, Grandpa always used to say..."

Chapter 94

Bill Chambers and Lance Reyes were there when Emily walked in the bar.

"Hey, over here!" Reyes said. "We pushed a couple of tables together for everybody. I hope we don't get kicked-out."

"I doubt it this time of day," Emily said. "They'll like the business. Hey, did you guys see the television this morning? With Murena?"

"No," Chambers said. "But I imagine his spinning things like a top, right?"

"Man!" Emily said. "It actually looks like he's going to get away with it, too. Unless…"

"Hey, there," Daryl Krebel said, "sorry I'm late. Made a wrong turn and ended up on the other side of the river somehow."

"The man knows weapons and tactics, but has always been weak on following directions," Reyes said.

"Sit down, Krebel," Chambers said. "I believe Graham here was about to lead us in a lecture about how politics works in the U. S. of A."

"I was just…" Emily said.

"Politics?" Daryl said. "Don't believe in it myself. Seems to always be more trouble than it's worth."

They laugh.

"So," Emily said. "You guys are okay with Murena doing what he's done, and ending up looking like some kind hero?"

"Graham," Chambers said.

"And the things he said!" Emily said. "He made it perfectly clear he's going to push even harder to make those changes that Klass wanted, just do it more sneaky-like."

"Sneaky-like," Chambers said. "Krebel, is that one of those tactical things Reyes says you're so good at?"

"I just meant…"

"I'm just yanking your chain, Graham," Chambers said. "Yes, the senator is just doing what all those people do when they get their, uh, when they get caught doing something. But, there's one major difference now."

"VanHollings?" Emily said.

"Right. He can spin things as much as he wants, but Adrianna VanHollings isn't there to make it work. It's just a matter of time now for Murena now. You watch and see."

"I still think..."

"Reyes," Daryl said. "You still remember where that off-switch is?"

Emily stared at Daryl.

"Hey," Emily said, "there's Angelique by the door. Be right back."

Emily walked over to where two people were talking with Angelique.

"We're just glad to see you are better," one of them said as they walked away.

"Miss Emily," Angelique said, "good morning."

"Morning, Angelique, I'm glad you could join us."

"Wouldn't miss it. Is that the group over at the tables?"

"Yeah, but, can I ask you a question before we go over there?"

"Sure, what is your question?"

"That little bag," she pulled the cloth bag from her pocket, "this one you gave me that day at your shop. What is it? I mean, is it another of those protection charms, or something like that? I guess it worked!"

"That," Angelique smiled. "Oh, no. Not protection. Did you look inside it."

"Yeah, I hope that's okay. It's just a picture."

"Yes, it's fine. It is a picture of Saint Mary Magdalene."

"Okay, yeah."

"She is the Saint that offers luck in love. It usually takes six months to work, but..."

"Six months?" Emily said. "To...find...love? It's a love charm? Is that what you're saying? I don't..."

"Hey, Graham!" Reyes said, "you to going to join us or do you want us to drag the tables over there?"

"Yeah," Emily said, "we're coming."

She looked at Angelique, as she put the bag back in her pocket.

"A love charm? Why in the world would you think I want...I mean..."

Angelique smiled.

"You just put it back in your pocket, didn't you?"

"Just go sit down." Emily said. "I mean. A love charm."

"What's got you all riled up now, Graham?" Chambers asked.

Emily just sat and shook her head.

"Hey," Daryl said, "now Bill found the off-switch. One of you need to tell me where it is."

Emily glared at Daryl. Then she saw the smile on Angelique's face.

"Hi everybody,"

"Hi Liz," Reyes said. "Pull up a seat. We're about to order drinks. What's everyone going to have? They're on Daryl here."

"Hey, now..." Daryl said.

"New guy buys." Reyes said. "You know the rules."

"Just some water for me, thanks."

"Water?" Daryl said. "You serious? We're in a bar, in New Orleans, and you want me to buy you water?"

"Yeah," Liz said. "Spring if they've got it."

"I can tell right now we're gonna need another off-switch," Daryl said.

"Oh," Liz said. "Dasilva said he'd be right in. He's outside on the phone. There he comes now."

"Everybody make room for the super agent," Emily said. "Did you get Manzaneres all taken care of?"

"Yes," Dasilva said. "Once he saw the bars he started talking and hasn't stopped. And Graham, about the super agent thing. I know what happened was lousy, and I wasn't able to do anything to stop it, but, maybe I can help ease it a bit this morning."

"Oh?" Emily said.

Dasilva set Emily's badge on the table.

"They're offering you your job back. With a promotion."

Everyone talked and offered congratulations until they looked at Emily.

"What's the matter?" Dasilva said. "Did I mention you were getting a promotion?"

"Yeah, you did," Emily said. "But you know, I've been thinking. After all that happened. Not you Arturo, I realize you were caught in all of it too. But I just don't think I want to go back in and deal with it again. I mean, tell me this, that stuff they did to you. Has all of that been taken care of yet. Have those people been dealt with?"

"No," Dasilva said. "There are still problems inside. But when you come back we can..."

"See, that's what I mean. I didn't want to be in the agency to spend my time trying to clean up the agency. And now, if it needs to be cleaned up, I think I can probably have a better shot at it from out here. I appreciate whatever you did Arturo, but thanks anyway. I'm not coming back."

"Can't honestly say that I blame you," Dasilva said. "If I thought I had other options I might do the same thing."

"Speaking of that," Reyes said. "Dasilva, I think Chambers has something to ask you."

"Ask me? What's that?"

Colonel Chambers leaned on the table facing Dasilva.

"Just this," Chambers said. "I have been working on something for a while now, and have now started putting it all together. I've already asked Reyes, and Daryl there, and they signed-on. Liz and Angelique too, they're all onboard. And now I'm asking you. I can't tell you all that much unless you do sign-on, but I'll just say we are creating a little group here that will spend its time dealing with things like happened two weeks ago. Oh, and like what is going on in your agency there, and in D. C. Interested?"

Dasliva looked at the others, then at Chambers.

"What do I need to sign?"

The others cheered.

"Wait a minute," Emily said. "Wait just a minute."

"What?" Reyes said.

"Colonel Chambers, I need to understand something."

"Here we go," Daryl said. "Ready with the switch, Reyes?"

"Okay, Graham. What is it?"

"A while back, after that boat thing, you announce that you had retired from all of this stuff. You were doing a few consulting things, but you were done with the military spy kind of stuff, the stuff you're talking about now. So, what's the deal? Is this another thing we're going to find out later was..."

"Graham!" Chambers said. "What is your problem? This isn't about something I said three years ago, not really. Why don't you tell me what is really eating at you?"

Emily stared.

"Reyes," Daryl said. "The switch! Find that switch!"

"What is it, Graham?"

"Okay, you want to know? I'll tell you. Why is it that, starting up this thing your doing, you ask Reyes to join, and the Cowboy there? Okay, I can understand that I guess, with all of their experience and stuff. But you asked Liz and Angelique. And now Dasilva! I mean, I don't have anything bad to say about any of them, but..."

"But why haven't I asked you to join, is that it? Is that what's bothering you?"

"Okay, yeah! Why didn't you ask me? What's the matter with me?"

"It's simple, Graham," Chambers said. "I thought it was a waste of time."

"A waste of…"

"Look at it," Chambers said. "Years ago, Munera asked you to join his outfit, and you said no. Not long ago VanHollings asked you to join her group, and you said no. Her kid asked you to join his group, and you said no. Dasilva just asked you to rejoin the agency, and you said no. Seems to me, Graham, that you just aren't a joiner. You prefer to do things on your own. Don't misunderstand. I have absolutely no problem with that. And you have the skills to make something of that approach. So, thinking it over, it just didn't make sense to me to waste the time asking. That's why."

Emily and Chambers looked at each other.

"So, because I said no to joining some half-brained groups ran by lunatics, and just said no to going back to the place that threw me out a month ago and the people who did it are still there, just because I said no to them you decided to not even give me the chance to join the group. Wow! Just Wow!"

"Alright, Graham. Maybe I was wrong. Maybe I misjudged you. Okay then. Emily, would you like to join our group here?"

Emily looked around the table at the smiles.

"No, thanks," Emily said.

"WHAT?" Chambers said. "Then what the hell was all that about…"

"Kidding! I'm kidding. I would be honored to be a part of this highly questionable group of highly skilled, but highly insane people."

"Graham!" Chambers said. "Sometimes you…"

"Wait!" Emily said. "Wait. There is one condition. One condition before I agree to join."

"Okay, Graham," Chamber said. "What is it?"

"I'll join up if magic stomach Krebel here agrees to drop the off-switch stuff."

Emily smiled.

"Consider it dropped," Reyes said. "Right Daryl?"

Silence.

"Right Daryl?"

"Yeah, okay. Dropped."

The group laughed, congratulated each other.

"I'll get the drinks," Daryl said.

"We'll help carry," Reyes said. "C'mon Graham."

They walked toward the bar.

"Be right back," Reyes said. "I need to use the can. Sorry, Graham."

Daryl gave the bartender the order and stood, looking around the room.

Emily noticed Angelique sitting at the table, smiling at her.

Emily looked out the window. She mumbled something to her self. She turned around and looked at Daryl.

"What?" he said.

"So, you come around here often, cowboy?" Emily said.

CONTACT INFORMATION

Visit J. B. Jamison's website at:
jbjamison.com

Facebook: @johnbjamison

distractionnovel.com
jamisonbooks.com

www.ingramcontent.com/pod-product-compliance
Lightning Source LLC
Chambersburg PA
CBHW030304200626
46816CB00002BA/753